"*Glorious Frazzled Beings* is storytelling magic — a haunting dream of a book, by turns strange and powerfully lucid. I'm captivated by the relations so boldly evoked. I'm moved by the intimacies, the wicked humour, the glorious dare of play. Angélique Lalonde is an original talent who is channeling forces far beyond us in this urgent debut." — David Chariandy, author of *Brother* and *I've Been Meaning to Tell You*

"Sly, mythical, wise, *Glorious Frazzled Beings* is an extraordinary work of non-conformist daring: a boy is born with fox ears, an abandoned pregnancy test is encountered by random women in mall bathroom, an overwhelmed mother makes clothing for tiny ghosts. With sharp visionary instinct, Lalonde not only confronts both the magic and cruelty of living, and the border between worlds, mythical and visceral — she lights it on fire. Brilliantly alive, full of devastation and wonder, reading these stories will change you." — Heidi Sopinka, author of *The Dictionary of Animal Languages*

"*Glorious Frazzled Beings* is a prophetic rhapsody of a book. Lalonde masterfully threads everyday magic through these stories, each a virtuoso exploration of what it means to be at home in the world we know, or the brave new world we are just discovering." — Christy Ann Conlin, author of *Watermark* and *The Speed of Mercy*

"From a garden in dawn's mist to the indignities of the dentist's chair, Lalonde's eclectic style penetrates the senses. With tremendous imagination, compassion, and fierce prose, these stories will walk you home." — Carleigh Baker, author of *Bad Endings*

"I love this book! A magical debut. Angélique Lalonde is one of those writers who is already absolutely brilliant. I can't believe she is just warming up. These are stories to curl around with a big mug of good tea, the kind of stories that seem lighthearted and whimsical but are actually doing so much heavy lifting. You will laugh out loud. You will find these lines embedded in your dreams, think of them while you are doing mundane chores, wonder at their sneaky magic — How did she do that? What is that spell? Sometimes you will think you have it figured out but ultimately, it will always elude you." — Katherena Vermette, author of *The Break* and *The Strangers*

Glorious Frazzled Beings

Angélique Lalonde

Published in Canada in 2021 and the USA in 2021 by House of Anansi Press Inc.
www.houseofanansi.com

House of Anansi Press is committed to protecting our natural environment. This book is made of material from well-managed FSC®-certified forests, recycled materials, and other controlled sources.

House of Anansi Press is a Global Certified Accessible™ (GCA by Benetech) publisher. The ebook version of this book meets stringent accessibility standards and is available to students and readers with print disabilities.

25 24 23 22 21   2 3 4 5 6

Library and Archives Canada Cataloguing in Publication

Title: Glorious frazzled beings / Angélique Lalonde.
Names: Lalonde, Angélique, author.
Description: Short stories.
Identifiers: Canadiana (print) 20210218630 | Canadiana (ebook) 20210218711 |
ISBN 9781487009571 (softcover) | ISBN 9781487009588 (EPUB)
Classification: LCC PS8623.A4475 G56 2021 | DDC C813/.6—dc23

Book design: Alysia Shewchuk
Cover artwork: Angélique Lalonde

House of Anansi Press respectfully acknowledges that the land on which we operate is the Traditional Territory of many Nations, including the Anishinabeg, the Wendat, and the Haudenosaunee. It is also the Treaty Lands of the Mississaugas of the Credit.

Canada Council Conseil des Arts
for the Arts   du Canada

ONTARIO ARTS COUNCIL
CONSEIL DES ARTS DE L'ONTARIO
an Ontario government agency
un organisme du gouvernement de l'Ontario

With the participation of the Government of Canada
Avec la participation du gouvernement du Canada | **Canadä**

We acknowledge for their financial support of our publishing program the Canada Council for the Arts, the Ontario Arts Council, and the Government of Canada.

Printed and bound in Canada

MIX
Paper from
responsible sources
FSC **FSC® C103567**
www.fsc.org

For all the glorious beings that have gifted me
with parts of their stories

Contents

Part One
Homemaking

Lady with the Big Head Chronicle

The lady with the big head is out there in the misty morning. Is she wearing a veil? What is she doing in my garden? The mist is sitting on the river, slightly spread over the land. I see the mountain beyond, and the lady with the big head stooped over my onions. Not like yesterday when the mist was so thick I wouldn't have seen her if she had been there.

Was she out there yesterday, picking calendula seeds to save for next season? She didn't ask me if she could tend my garden while I was in the house doing other things. She's never talked to me at all. She avoids me if I try to approach her, floating off into the mist or the memory of mist, then reappearing later doing different things in different places. I saw her digging at an anthill with the bear that has been hanging around our yard. She used a stick and the bear used her big broad paws.

The lady with the big head was helping the bear, or the bear was helping the lady with the big head, I'm not sure which. Either way, they were digging up the anthill near the apple tree. I didn't mind that. I had noticed the ants were in the sickly tree crawling all around and that probably was not a good sign, so maybe the lady with the big head and the bear were helping the apple tree too.

She might be taking some onions, or weeding, or eating slugs. I can't tell exactly what she is doing because the veil that hangs down from her big head drapes over her body to the ground and hides her movements. Also the light has not yet come, only a faint blueness and all that mist. I could offer her a hot tea but if I walk out there she'll float away from me.

Later I'll go look and see if she has taken onions or left any knick-knacks. Once I found a spool of golden thread so strong, fine, and shiny, I knew it was magical. The kind of thread that could be used to build spiderwebs that are always visible no matter the light. Visible but still translucent, an ephemeral quality of there and not quite there, only gold instead of silver. It might be what she makes her veil out of, or at least what she uses to mend the veil, because now that I think of it the veil is not golden, it's more of a purple-grey shadow. Sometimes she has it pulled back and I can almost make out her features as she goes about doing things ladies with big heads do. She looks a little bit like me and a little bit like Rod Stewart, which is an odd mix for a lady. A couple of times I've glimpsed her looking like my dog, John Black, who died last winter. She might have taken her skull from the forest, where we left the dog's body, to use as a mask; it seems like something the lady with the big head would do.

Lady with the big head and the weight of her head

The lady with the big head is having trouble holding her head up. It's dipping forward this week, jutting at the chin. A chiropractor would look at her and shudder, thinking of her unhappy spine, contorted and compressed by the heaviness of gravity. He would want to brace her somehow, crack her in all sorts of places, and have her do little exercises with devices of his own making to relieve the pressure on her neck.

Who can she consult for this, living as she does in the forest? Being only partway real? Who would book her in for an appointment with her lack of proper name and no address to speak of? No email or phone number to confirm a correct time? Who would make a call to the forest, following her trail to find where she is sleeping and wrench that crook from her neck? How would she pay them? Would a chiropractor accept dried mushrooms in payment for his services? Would he treat without an X-ray showing the insides of the lady with the big head's troubled bones?

Instead we build her a device from which she can hang upside down, with a long flat back that inverts once she's strapped herself in. I hang there a lot when she's not using it, feeling the blood pool in my head, imagining my spine unkinking so more of my life can bubble up through that crazy central nerve cluster that sends messages all through my body, making it so I can know.

Lady with the big head has a dream

She had a quiet dream, the lady with the big head. It was quiet so she kept sleeping. If it had been a loud raucous dream she would have startled herself out of it. She does not want to dream raucous dreams. Still, sometimes she does. She seeps in my window and makes me dream them too.

She dreams she is living in a musty apartment where the shower runs straight onto the carpet and there are old patio umbrellas stacked in the storeroom. Enough of them that there is no room to store her own things. There are also a few toilets side by side, some of them with equipment attached to them for various kinds of disabilities. The lady with the big head does not want to live in this apartment. She wipes up dust and pubic hair gathered around the toilets that was not cleaned away before she moved in. She wonders why she is paying rent here when it has not been cleaned of other people's pubic hair, and the landlord is storing things in her storeroom. There are two bathtubs side by side in another part of the apartment, one slightly lower than the other. The lower one has a rack in it like a water-bath canner and is very dirty. The lady with the big head pours two baths and gets in the cleaner one. She seems happy to have a bath in the dream. She is in the bath with a friend who is living down the hall and tells her not to get in the lower bath because it is filled with other people's filth.

Later the lady with the big head wakes up and goes around the forest. She doesn't live in a musty apartment. She doesn't have a bath and there is soil everywhere. It does not seem soiled. She goes down to the cold river and washes her face. Some of it washes right off. The lady with the big head is going around with only part of a face today, refreshed to be kept so clean by the world. A new face will grow back; it always does. Who knows what it will look like. Part of her face will look like her old face and part of her face will be her new face. She follows the cycle of the moon. As the moon wanes the rest of her old face will peel off in fragments. In the darkest night of the new moon she'll be wiped clean of that old face and her new face will be there, coming to fruition over the next few weeks toward some kind of whole. During full moon she glows with the fullness of her features, distinct for such a short window of time. If you didn't already know her by the size of her head, you'd know her then by the flicker and fullness of her face.

Lady with the big head knits

The lady with the big head has started a new knitting project. She has gathered mycelia from the undersides of leaves, dried it, weaving in lichens hanging from pine trees, grasses dried before they harden too much to be malleable, licks of the thinnest birch and hazel branches. All strung together and rolled into balls. The lady with the big head is knitting a fine gown and a warm blanket. She is knitting a scarf and toque for the mangy squirrel that lost much of its coat to mites this summer. She gathers bits of feather and tufts of fur scattered in the forest from fresh coyote kills, along the roadside from smashed-up deer and grouse. These she loops in for warmth and softness amongst the brittle structures of plant and fungus parts.

Lady with the big head pilfers garlic

The lady with the big head is digging a hole for the winter. Last year's burrow collapsed because of all the rain. She has borrowed our shovel, which we had hoped to use to prepare the ground for garlic. The lady with the big head mostly leaves the garlic alone. We put out a few bundles in the barn so that she will not dig up our seed. One year we lost almost our whole harvest to her, but we learned that if we made an offering she would leave the stuff in the ground alone.

She wants us to have our garlic but if there is not enough to go around she will pilfer. She needs the garlic to keep her belly warm over the long winter. To spice up the plain roots she keeps stored in her caches and the cambium she munches in leaner times.

The lady with the big head knows how to make fires. Probably she knows how to start them from flints, but she also takes matches and lighters. Either it's her or our son William, who is trying to hide his pyrotechnic activities. William assures us he's seen her smoking whatever brand of cigarettes she can get her hands on and tossing the butts under the pine tree where she thinks no one will see them. When we buy a three-pack of strike-anywheres from the hardware store we always leave a pack sealed in a zip-lock out in the barn in the cubby set aside for offerings, to make things a little easier for her.

Sometimes she leaves things for us in return—bits of woven grass or the skeletons of small animals, any garbage William tosses out in the bush with his friends when they're out there being dickheads. Probably they think it's funny that the lady with the big head will pick up after them. But we warn them to be careful, as she's not a custodian. She has a streak of righteousness to her, and one way or another, we tell William, something bad will come of his carelessness if he keeps goading her.

Lady with the big head reads poetry

Does the lady with the big head suffer from heartburn? It is hard to say because her body is such a mystery. Perhaps that big head weighs down on her organs, making acid rise up her esophagus to burn her throat. Or perhaps because of her healthful diet of herbs, roots, plants, and small animals, she is safe from such refluxes. One thing we know is that the lady with the big head is a big admirer of poetry. We leave volumes for her in the barn because she knows better than to accept gifts from us directly. In the beginning when we left books out she would take them and not bring them back. We lost several of our favourite poets that way and are still uncertain where they've gone. There would be no way for her to keep the books from rotting out there with all the dampness. Without insulated walls and ongoing fires or electric baseboard heaters things out there won't keep. They'll rot and rust and be taken over by mosses, their original words and functions becoming unreadable. So even if she has kept them, they are still lost to us, and will become lost to her also. Unless of course she is able to commit them to memory, which is highly possible with that big head of hers that must have so much room in it for stories about the world.

We have long discussions in our home about what volume to offer up next, how to pick poets for the lady with the big head's attunement to the literary world. William writes out pages of his favourite hip-hop rhymes so that she'll be in the know about different kinds of verse, not just filled up with the tender shit his mothers are into. She leaves us the spectres and voices of the nonhuman to learn as we leave her the weavings of those who play and build with the language the colonizers left us. Who knows how many misunderstandings pass between us? And truthfully we have no education in poetry. Only the internet and the suggestions put forth by the surveillance of our previous choices to offer us other things we might like based on the things we have chosen before. Also a pitiful section of poetry in our local library, which nonetheless we are grateful for. Sometimes our friends will send us things from the cities in which they live where human words sprawl over the landscape. Here many of those words are washed away or covered in brush as soon as they arrive, unable to convey the poets' observations about human-scale land- scapes and being. The land here eats everything. There are after all so many intact spirits roaming, and they are hungry for knowing. The lady with the big head is a little bit like a medium between us and this world. We fumble toward knowing one another with our gifts and intentions, undaunted by our failures to understand—thrilled by the revelations that come.

Lady with the big head shares her kill

It is unclear whether or not the lady with the big head has children. Many creatures follow her around and participate in her doings. Two ravens perch in a poplar to watch her handiwork as she cuts across the grouse's neck and holds its feet to rip the skin off. She keeps the breasts and feathers and tosses the rest of it to the ravens. She's not greedy, makes sure to share what she is gifted from the world.

After ripping as much flesh as they can get, the ravens get wind of another kill, take off in the direction of death. The lady with the big head continues wandering, tomorrow she plans to spend all day at the river reading rocks, testing the words of lichen with her practised tongue.

Lady with the big head's sexuality

The lady with the big head was not human before she became a partway ghost, which is why I chide Alma, calling her "my prudish wife," when she is disgusted by the lady with the big head's sexuality. This morning after licking dew from cabbage fronds, the lady with the big head fornicated with a giant raven in the yard, making us think maybe she consorts with gods. Her screams had us rushing outside, thinking the cat had been attacked by coyotes.

William got out his smart phone, trying to make a video, but luckily we were on him before he could make it to the cell booster for a signal. We confiscated the phone and erased any traces of an encounter that was never meant to be made into media, then had a good talk about respecting people's boundaries. He argued that the lady with the big head and the raven were not really people and if they were they should be a little more discreet about where they decided to fuck.

We reminded William that despite legal title, we're encroaching on territory that has boundaries chronicled in stories that have never been told to us, and maybe the lady with the big head is part of that world. Or maybe she isn't. There is so much we cannot know because of the knowledge we have been born into, passed down through the direct or banal violence of our immigrant ancestors. It may be that she has been here so very long, as ancient as the land. Or perhaps she came with us or with some other settlers from another part of the world, got marooned here, and goes on living even though the humans that once knew her are gone or dead and their children do not remember. We do not know how to ask, or who to ask, and the lady with the big head is not telling. But William is fourteen and immersed in dominant cultural values (despite our best efforts) so he doesn't get these discrepancies. He's all over what's mine and not mine, thinking you can really own things, that legal possession gives you alienable rights that exclude other truths from the land. Alma isn't sure how the lady with the big head's sexual life will affect William's burgeoning sexuality. This morning it was the raven and last week we saw her sensually stroking a vixen's back, the purr from her throat unmistakable. Alma's been keeping William inside lately because of the birchbark etchings that have been popping up on the trails. The kind of images that make me shiver down there, making me so uncomfortably aroused that shame clamps me down before the pleasure can spread any further. The lady with the big head depicts the erotic life of forest creatures in ways that enliven our human erogenous zones. We find ourselves arguing in bed about whether she is being vulgar or artful out there in the forest all around.

Lady with the big head's perspective on identity

The lady with the big head does not really care about technologies of identity construction and the limited dialectics of culture inherent in dominant practices of person-making. Meaning comes to her through languages of texture and heeding. Quick-sight-and-categorize is not the primary way she has learned to become among others like or unlike her. Therefore she categorizes differently.

There are so many ways of likeness.

The lady with the big head interrelates intimately with many beings and because of this the plain sufferings of humans fall in line with the plain sufferings of salmon, hummingbird, lichen, salamander, and snail.

Watching her out there limping I can see that the lady with the big head has become very angry that the plain sufferings of salmon have become so much less plain through the grasping patriarchy of capital and conquest, as we go on taking and taking and taking from this world in the drive to constantly remake ourselves.

The lady with the big head is listening for silenced voices. Sometimes I wish she would start yelling in a big ghost voice that causes terrible reverberations to frighten away surveyors who fly around in helicopters trying to decide how to pipe bitumen and gas under the land to put in big leaky ships across oceans so that more cheap plastic goods can be manufactured to accumulate dangerously in the world. That her voice had the power to change this.

But maybe that's just me, inventing motivations and capabilities for her. Maybe in my looking I am like others like me — an accident or designed outcome of the generations that came before. Left here with garbled stories because each generation tries to efface or correct the stories of the last in our attempts to settle ourselves. The stories that bind us to place transformed with each displacement. Solid as we claim ourselves to be, we are deeply unsure what to do with the buried stories that froth forth into our fields of perception. Stories that link us uncomfortably to the violent displacements that have made this home. We writhe with our inability to make meaning as the lady with the big head voyages along the dendritic trails of her manifold histories.

Lady with the big head intuits ice

The lady with the big head intuits ice as a long pause in the body of the world. She knows it's not really like that because ice is dynamic, changing itself constantly as the world around it fluctuates, loosening its bonds and flowing away or tightening toward itself and heaving into space. Marching to cover land masses and bust open rock. Not really a self at all, able to exist as water or vapour. Becoming forceful and epic, becoming vastness, becoming the body of the world, breaking the body of the world into infinitesimal fragments which it devours or gestates. Always in flux with the stuff that makes land.

The lady with the big head tries to parse out the spirit bits. The enlivened elements. She sticks her hand into ice and has to pull back because it's just so cold! She sticks her hand into water and animalcules cling to her, blotching her skin, nibbling her cells. The water is so inviting she plops herself in, grateful for a big head that floats like a buoy. Her limbs fall below, but her breathing hole must be kept out or water will clog her and push out her spirit, turning her body to fodder. She cannot live in water, cannot live without water. So unlike salamander, who doesn't need to keep constant temperature, and like salamander, too — rhythmically heaved by breath. She reaps the benefits of pulse. But because she is only somewhat alive she can pause herself like ice for eons, fragmented, covering up the cities we made that we thought would last forever, turning them into questions for future creatures that come after the ice.

Lady with the big head tells me to shut the fuck up

I think I hear the lady with the big head whispering. Maybe she is telling me to shut the fuck up? Not for just one hot second, or three timed minutes registered in my meditation app and logged online to be compared with others like me who have become so aware of their mindfulness? Maybe she just keeps saying shhh, shhhh, shhhh, like we used to whisper to William when he was a baby and crying all the time, needing to be soothed by his mothers' warm soft breaths? Maybe she is saying that it is so hard to hear when we are always stating things, crashing about the multi-voiced world with our so-loud authoritative claims and combustion-engine machinery?

then it goes that you get real quiet for a real long time,
no one knows how long, and there are a lot of things you hear,
and then maybe after a long time
there is a sound that moves you.

not like moving in your limbs to get things done, but another kind of moving
    — one that comes from inside the body, real deep in there.

maybe a little bit close inside between the lungs and heart
where there is all that breathing and blood pumping
            and there you get moved, still real quiet
                    because you're trying not to make it about
                    your words and your knowing
                    make place for another kind of being
like moving *with* instead of moving *about*.

you're out there in her garden and she's making a hole with her fingers in the soil.
    you've got to respect her veil but it's hard not to want so much to peek inside.
        you tease apart the root bulb, hand her one piece
            then another. she is asking you only to break up the bulb
            and hand her the parts one by one.
            she is not moving away from you
            as long as you break up the bulb
        and hand her the parts one by one.
            (without pressing your narratives in,
                assuming you might know
                    how to know her world.)

The Town Carmen Found

Carmen Alendra found an old town in the woods behind her house one day. A town that hadn't been there every other time she had walked the back field to the pond. At first it seemed it was just one old house she hadn't noticed, but as she went through the old house, finding antique bottles and tableware covered in dust, things shifted. She opened cupboards and bent down low to look at bottom shelves, walked through doors that led to other doors and out of the first house onto the walkway of the next. Carmen roamed through the town, finding neat rows of small modest houses that seemed to have been inhabited and abandoned sometime between 1930 and 1955.

One of the houses was slightly bigger, with a high ceiling. In this building there were dishes and decorations all up the walls—metal colanders and forms hanging thirty feet up, an old wooden cookstove in the corner, and dusty linens that had once been starched crisp draped on the windowsills. The door off the kitchen led to a big open room with chalkboards on the walls and a hardwood floor that Carmen surmised must have been the schoolroom. There were big bright windows letting in armfuls of astonishing light, and Carmen Alendra danced. She danced in the room in a way she had never danced before, becoming light and mobile, bending, branching, tracing out the beauty of something corporeal, secret, and clear. Despite her everyday heaviness, Carmen soared. She swirled and dipped and leaped in that room—joyful, free, unencumbered.

Although things were falling apart slightly from disuse in the town and there were bats in the cupboards and torn-up wallpaper where squirrels had been munching, Carmen thought her happiness might lie in fixing a place for herself among all the old dusty things of another time.

Carmen could feel that there were other lives happening simultaneously in hidden corners of the town. Although the inhabitants had left the space, she would catch traces of them, sense that they had been there just moments ago and now no longer were: little workshops on desks where small books were being manufactured, a drawer with old lamps that someone was fixing up, plans for turning the courtyard into an ice-skating rink come winter.

With one exception, Carmen never saw anyone when she visited. She was superstitious about the town, and although she longed to live there permanently, she had a sense that if she changed things, even if she just tidied up a bit, the whole town would disappear—and Carmen wanted more than anything just to keep discovering. So she visited and danced among the dust, a creature of light and movement. She pulled trinkets out and put them back and each time she went she discovered things she'd never seen.

The one time she wasn't alone in the town was the morning she encountered a lover in one of the small outbuildings filled with paper, boxes, and wooden shelves. They whispered and grasped each other, familiar yet foreign. Somehow they both happened to be there at the same time, and this sparked an eroticism in her that was like the dance in the schoolroom, only the body of another moved alongside hers, releasing sparks of immeasurable delight. She didn't look for the lover again, knowing it was part of the town's magic. This too was just one of her moments of discovery, different but linked to the lamp parts in the drawer of the tiny house on the upslope; the squat green hut with drawers of all shapes and sizes furnished only with a frayed dinosaur rug askew on an uneven floor.

The town Carmen found was always ravelling and unravelling itself, and in this it was like Carmen, who was like all living creatures: a continuous compendium of death, regeneration, joy, fear, waste, and fury. She longed for things and when she was not longing, longed for longing itself. Unlike those of strong faith, she was not content to serve others, to continuously give in service of an ideal.

Spiritual fulfillment did not come for her from the crevasses of humanity. Carmen's spirit was filled in the dream world, in her forest wanders, and the town Carmen found was rife with the stuff in which spirit could flourish, embedded thickly in the divine. Oh behold! she would exclaim in empty rooms wearing all the trappings of their inhabitants' messy lives. Alas, the glory! Bells ringing through the air, soft kisses of a humanity we wish for but otherwise fail to manifest. Quiet in the spaces between—absurdly and tenderly beautiful.

The town Carmen found was a stained-glass window in a thirteenth-century gothic cathedral, light of the morning shining through on worshippers filled with awe; transcendent pleasure extended by the gaze of a terrible loving sovereign.

⁓

Is it useful here to describe piece by piece the time Carmen was given in the town that she found? To draw a contrast between that world, and the other Carmen inevitably had to return to? The world of food, sleep, dirty dishes needing to be washed, exhaust pipes, mousetraps that she baited, set, and emptied on a weekly basis, parasitic fungi, books on faith written by racist men, policy manuals for big-box-store employees, safety videos, and certificate programs for the unemployed?

In the town Carmen found, bereft of human interlocutors, none of these things clung to her. Even the lover had been so vocally silent. Just the body, the inspirited body making sound! In the town Carmen found, she was light, a swift traveller passing through the soft remnants of someone else's dreams. And these dreams, unlike her own, left her filled with magnificent residues of love. Cracked open, she became some other Carmen — not the awkward, gawking creature she saw reflected in storefront windows walking intently with a crook to her neck, societal burdens weighing heavily on her spine. In the town Carmen found she was lithe and painless, every expression a performance of a being in perfect harmony with the beauty of the world.

Like any other creature in a story, in the town Carmen found she became flat. Losing edges to the page, the painful parts of her story carved off, shed like dead skin on a wet towel. The loathsome bits left for microscopic insects with mouthpieces specialized for dead human cells.

But was this necessary for Carmen to dance? Or was it just a dance of a different order, this free movement in abandoned rooms? Surfacing, being submerged, body unmarred by the weight of time? Was it necessary for this Carmen to be juxtaposed with day-to-day Carmen — the beloved with the banal, the spirit with the body? Was it necessary to split Carmen into two to achieve transcendence? Didn't transcendence itself require something to overcome, some lightness of being excavated from a sodden substrate?

In the town Carmen found there was evidence of vast decay yet this did not hinder Carmen's heart. She found spaciousness within it. Carmen invited Douglas but they could not find the town. Then she invited Rupert and the town was there but Rupert focused on the price he could get for some of these goods on eBay. Rupert and Carmen tried to dance but the effect was comical rather than rapturous. He was shy about his body, couldn't stop thinking about what he looked like to Carmen, what she thought of him while he moved. Carmen picked up his awkwardness and felt stunted. With Sheila Joffers it was the same thing, and after that Carmen stopped bringing friends along to the town because she couldn't hear it speak when they were speaking. Human speech drowned out those other ephemeral symbols. Still, she harboured a hope that there would be other recognizable dancers, that she would meet them in the world and that they would dance together, unhindered by the space between selves.

Once, Carmen Alendra went to the town following a particularly gruelling information session on hereditary law. She did her taxes, ate a poppy seed bagel, downed a carafe of healthful tea, and headed back into the woods. This produced a twitching kind of dance in which her mind dive-bombed her kneecaps, so she was constantly flopping back. Carmen twitched and turned, banging into the floor and walls, and this too was a kind of ecstatic expression. She called it "the tax man," and for a season it became big in Reykjavik when Carmen travelled there and attended some discotheques. People liked the flail of it, how it wiggled all sorts of tensions out of them. Being beat up by and beating the tax man all at the same time.

The town Carmen found would not have been so remarkable if it had been the same as the rest of the world. This led Carmen to infer that there must be boundaries around the sacred. She just wasn't sure who set them. If she understood quantum-level realities she might have been drawn to questions of beauty at the heart of nature. If she understood faith she might easily have ascribed all goodness to the Creator's hand. If she were a mathematically minded being of faith, she might see these premises as equal. If Carmen believed in the generative power of her own visions she might then place herself as the maker. But like so many of us in this day and age, Carmen was wishy-washy. She'd get close to understanding and it would fade from her to be replaced by some other possibility. And each possibility remained possible for her so that she could never quite decide what she should believe firmly and was therefore unable to articulate a larger vision for anything. She accepted things as they were while they were there, longed after manufactured ideals, and mourned her losses bitterly.

The town was remarkable because Carmen recognized her happiness there. For a time she dove full force into the

face of joy. Fortitude and grace marked her, a happiness
leashed to a temporary gift.

⁓

Carmen Alendra lost an old town in the woods behind her
house one day. She went back and back and back for days,
trying to find it. She went back repeatedly over many years,
but that town that Carmen had found was only a limited-
time thing.

The town Carmen had found defined her for the rest of
her life, even though she could only go there in memory. In
finding the town, Carmen had learned that a place existed
in which she could simply be. A place where there were no
gaps to her, where her deepest hopes were realized — hopes
she didn't even know she had.

When Carmen lost the town, and for a long time after,
she felt she could never feel whole again. She kept trying
to figure out how to be in an everyday world in which she
was often lost, but without the town to get back to and
find herself in, she kept getting tripped up by sticks in the
spokes of her wheels. Life kept throwing punches at her,
like it was punishing her somehow for the perfection she'd
inhabited in the town that she found in the woods behind
her house one day.

How do you get up time and time again, Carmen? How
do you go on when your memory calls you back to the way

things were and the only thing you want is the you that you were then? When every word from your mouth seems tied to the loss of what was?

Here is Carmen sitting at a window drawing detailed plans of the town as it was every time she went there. Here is Carmen writing a diary about what she saw. Here is Carmen trying to dance, ordering antiques online to design her house the way she saw in the town that she found. Here is Carmen hiding in cupboards full of paper, boxes, and wooden shelves touching herself all over the way that lover did, pretending her hands are not hers. Here is Carmen trying to stay hopeful, despite the loss of the town. Carmen files paperwork. Carmen watches videos; Carmen eats noodles in broth; Carmen walks around in the woods, looking for another way in, pretending she is just walking in the woods and not looking for a way in.

～

Looking back after the shock of grief, Carmen would see all the layers of her pretending, all the incantations she tried to bring the magic back. She frazzled in the bowels of her grief for a good long while, coming out somewhat composted on the inside. No longer so lithe, no longer so young, Carmen had more layers to her. A soil test would have told her she'd become a more balanced ecosystem, ground in which a greater diversity could thrive.

Carmen turned to literature to parse out the pain. Slowly she began to talk. Carmen talked to Sheila Joffers, who it turned out had lost a twin sister to suicide. Both Sheila and her sister Pomona had battled the dark demons of their seemingly severed selves, diagnosed at twelve and eleven as clinically depressed. Although the antidepressants had got them through adolescence, Pomona wanted to know herself outside of chemical regulation, drawn by curiosity to the innate sparks of her mind. Pomona hurdled in and out of the darkness through her twenties, and at thirty-two ripped her wrists open with their mother's kitchen shears.

Two years Sheila spent in a group home after Pomona's burial, her bereaved family certain Sheila would be next. Sparkly little Sheila, who would have guessed it? Always doing everything right, and cheerful to the bone. Carmen pegged her for an all-together type, figured she had been unable to dance with her because of her uptightness. When they dug into it, Carmen learned that Sheila had been afraid, uncertain in Carmen's town how to partake, despite her desire to dance the way Carmen did.

Rupert too had his failures. Ambiguous about being a caring man in this world, he ached for tenderness and found freedom only in the expression of rage and competitive advantage. Rupert wanted to make it and hated the system at the same time. Unable to love, Rupert wanted to sell or smash things, acquire or destroy. He was unable to find any worth in things other than the way they figured into his own wanting. Still, when he was able in rare moments to rest he saw the truth of his longing. Rupert told Carmen he had been jealous of her town, jealous of her joy, wanted to claim it for himself and hated her for finding it and showing it to him, revealing the poverty of his separation.

Carmen learned each soul has a troubled story, isolated in the myth of its own loneliness. When she paused her own seeking she was able to listen deeply. She heard the little voices of these other beings and her heart was educated by them.

The town taught Carmen Alendra about rapture; through grief Carmen learned there's a deeper beauty, but it's not personal.

Carmen Alendra stumbled through loss and found another route home. It was not the home she would have wanted for herself, had you asked her when she was young and all wrapped up in an old town. This home was all crumpled up in some places, full of life's accruements. There were no besotted lovers in her daily bed, no perfect matches for her clever self, no volumes of her memoirs causing a literary stir. No perfect arrangement of things that didn't somehow crumble. When she was lucky, some squirrels up to antics out the window, a bowl of fruit revealed in light, a letter from a friend in the mailbox, a story in a good book that caught her heart in her throat to make her look at the world anew. Sometimes bending and breathing a certain way she would feel the world as a calm unfolding through her body.

Through the complex web of embodied joys, refusals, rejections, and sorrows, Carmen encountered a town on the inside of her being, a town that could be shared without pain of rupture. A town in which communion became possible. Carmen learned to navigate time and schism through the vehicle of breath. Energetic doorways clicked open, revealing an ancestral vastness. There she found sadness and rupture, and beneath that a calm tender warmth. Her senses travelled the silk channels of an inward web, revealing a piezoelectric garden. And here Carmen learned to embrace, rather than steel herself against the vibrational frequencies of joy, fear, anxiety, and hunger.

Turning inward Carmen learned to calm the fuck down, ride the waves out, whatever the force they carried. Instead of getting rigid, Carmen allowed for her fascial webs to transduce, passing the force along and out to wherever it might need to go. Carmen stopped storing fear. Grief like a flood left her. Raw, empty Carmen, just like the old rooms. All the buildups she had gathered in the pass down from life to life, her organism carrying the gummy blindness of hereditary time, learning how to be a woman from social strictures set up to tear her spirit down, keep her body in line. In her calmness Carmen learned to love. There was tenderness for Rupert, tenderness for Sheila Joffers, tenderness for Carmen Alendra, all mumbling about in inspirited flesh.

Malarkey

Marianne Thickenson is exploring her spirituality. She is thirty-eight years old and childless, focused until now on making something of herself. Remaining childless and (theoretically) independent has given Marianne a lot of playing room in her explorations. For the last few years, however, her carnal life has become frenziedly driven by hormonal impulses quite different from those that made her want to rub her body against all sorts of soft and rigid things when her breasts plumped out and hair forced itself out of hitherto hairless body parts as an adolescent girl.

Back then it was all made sense of through romantic ideas about love and destiny but lately there's been an aching pulse in her womb that feels like a spirit trying to rip through the fabric of the universe seeking insemination in order to be made flesh.

Marianne wants to live rightly in the world but was not raised with any kind of guiding morality to fall back on with certainty; therefore she looks for guidance everywhere. For Marianne chance encounters offer spiritual revelation. She picks up cues from random conversations between strangers that she happens to overhear. Particular hot spots include lineups at the grocery store, the movie theatre, the credit union, the tire shop, cafés and bus stops. She also jots quotes down from radio programs, Instagram, and podcasts about books and the people who write them. Marianne makes her own interpretations.

Once she heard a woman with black hair and long red nails wearing dream catcher earrings talking to a boy about kindness. She wrote in her journal:

> Be nice to your friends, let it mean something. Be kind
> and good-hearted. Give lovingly without longing for
> return. Be kind to your friends, do not pull at their hair
> and kick them, offer them snacks just to take them
> back, or give them snacks and complain afterwards
> that they have taken from you.

Marianne holds fast to this. It allows her to go on living with Dev LaRue. If you asked she would tell you that she loves him like a sheep loves clover: wrapped into its tongue and pushed sideways, mashed into sweet liquid green and fibre in the crush of its grinding teeth. Marianne

Thickenson wants to suck every sweetness from him, excrete the indigestible in little pellets that feed the soil so it can keep growing the goodness of clover on which they can both feed. As his sweetness passes through her, tingling her from the inside, she feels a sense of closeness with the goodness of God's creation.

~

She loves Dev but often wants to take back the things she has given because she feels like she has given too much and he has not given as much or even been aware of what she has given. Marianne wants to smash her special friend with everyday household objects sometimes because he believes he deserves to be cared for without needing to care back.

Meanwhile Dev LaRue is interested in global politics and sword-craft. He would like to brandish weaponry like back in the day when *katanas* were slung across ninjas' backs. His interest in politics is cursory; he picks up bits of information from the national broadcaster and identifies with callers on the afternoon talkback show who say things loudly and don't get emotional about what they are saying. "It's got to be rational," he tells Marianne when she says that she gets someone's point even when they're choked up about it and get defensive or say contradictory things that don't necessarily match up with the stance the radio host is prodding them into.

Dev says "love you too, babe" to Marianne, but he doesn't really care about love, he just wants her to know he's attached to her and has learned over the course of many emotional fallouts that it's important for her to think that he loves her so she goes on loving him. Dev LaRue is interested in himself and the way he pictures his life. He is attached to Marianne because he thinks he knows what to expect of her and she doesn't make life too difficult for him most of the time. Every once in a while she goes on a tangent of fury and criticizes him for not fulfilling her expectations. The furies usually pass and she settles back into good humour after she feels they've had a good talk. Marianne retreats for a while, reads things in her books and then comes back to Dev and prods, trying to understand where he's coming from and explain in rational language how the things he has done or not done have hurt her. Most of the time it bothers him from the work he is doing with his art supplies to invent worlds of fulfillment, intrigue, adrenalin, and glory, and he must muster every ounce of patience not to resent these intrusions into the clashing and crafting of blades.

Dev is on volume 4 of a seven-volume graphic novel fantasy series set on an alien planet called Malarkey in the galaxy Tesalon III — a series he intends to publish in its entirety once he has finished all seven volumes. "Malarkey," he says to Marianne in a deadpan voice — spreading his hands out before him to communicate an expanse of

monumental proportions brought into being by the force
of his imagination — "where time-travelling extraterrestrial roamers captured and deposited seven villages of earth
people from various parts of the planet during different
historical periods and put them all together at distances
far enough that they could maintain a certain degree of
isolation, but close enough that they would eventually have
to interact with one another."

The extraterrestrial overseers are never depicted visually
in Dev's books, but traces of their interference are revealed
to the reader via hand-lettered papyrus scrolls discovered
by the people in their various languages (translated into
English in footnotes) at various sacred sites when the Gods
want to interact with the humans they keep for entertainment purposes.

In Dev's narrative the reader is meant to follow the stick-
and sword-wielding heroic humans living out their lives via
sequential boxes meant to represent viewing screens on the
extraterrestrial home world. Woven into the narrative are
fan ratings for the extraterrestrial viewers "watching" the
drama play out on their screens. When fan ratings fall, the
fictional producers introduce new elements of technology
or novel geological events into lives that have become too
predictable, complacent, or peaceful to make good viewing. Fires, earthquakes, volcanoes, floods, insect rampages,
famines, warfare, the invention of the wheel, the revelation
of metallurgy to a group of Wiru from the highlands of

New Guinea (allowing Dev the creative freedom of design-
ing what a culturally contextual Wiru sword might have
looked like), out-group liaisons causing blending, diaspora,
and social upheaval are all motifs that have been explored.

Dev spends a lot of time researching and modifying
different kinds of swords from different societies in human
history. He wants there to be historical accuracy in his
fantasy world. It's important for him that he gets the facts
right before he starts experimenting with them. His extra-
terrestrials are like that too; they don't introduce things to
their humans that would have been too far-fetched for the
generative populations of earth humans from which they
drew their stock. Dev thinks it's a clever contrast because
the humans he's placed under extraterrestrial surveillance
on Malarkey remain historically accurate with creative
flairs thrown in for narrative purposes, while earth, in
his saga, has evolved into an interconnected globe united
under a single political system referred to by its people as
Pangea II. It has progressed into a futuristic heterotopia
("both u- and dis-topic elements manifesting through
various subplots," Dev likes to imagine coining to hosts
of book interviewers asking about his clever imaginaries).
A computer-animal-human-interfaced society in which
androids, humans, and humanimals have just received legal
rights to marry.

Dev spent an entire month working on a pullout center-
fold poster for volume 4. A stunning watercolour wedding

portrait of the first humanimal-android spousal unit using Marianne's graduation headshot superimposed on an Audubon backend of a tiptoeing doe as the blueprint for the bride. She stands with her backcombed hairspray-stiff hair gallantly framing her nubile face, neon elastics in glistening metallic braces — as though she were a futuristic space vessel set to flight by the sails of a sixteenth-century ship, bound for the magnificent unknown. Her hoof rests tenderly in the hand of an android that looks unambiguously like a hulked and handsome gold-skin version of his pal Leon. Who incidentally Marianne had a short-lived affair with during the creation of volume 2. An affair that had ended sloppily, with Marianne telling Dev she didn't want to see Leon's face again because he was a boorish pig who had no respect for women. Dev, so engrossed in a brutal war between the newly emerged Yan Dynasty and a powerful Ossonubo Chieftaincy (both Malarkey originals!), had not even noticed her emotional flourishing, repentance, disillusionment, and anger throughout the course of the summer intrigue. He assumed that it had been Leon's misogynistic analysis of the U.S. president's latest tweet during wing night at Su Lin's Bar and Grill that had fostered Marianne's vengeful loathing.

Marianne is working on loving Dev even when he does not really look at her for days, just mutters stock phrases like "sweet dreams" and "ciao babe" on his way to the bathroom when he notices she's making preparations for sleep or leaving the house for work. She is working on loving his charming inclusions of a fantasy her in his fantasy world, while continuing to harbour illusions that because he includes her in his fantasies he might learn to fulfill her needs.

These illusions surface in the most surprising of moments even though Marianne has learned (painfully) over the course of the decade she has loved him that Dev's interest in her, like his interest in politics, is only cursory. Her spiritual inquiries have taught her that desiring Dev to change into a person who loves her as she needs to be loved is a clear and persistent path to perpetual unhappiness. Hence the sometimes rage. Because although Marianne Thickenson has learned this, she often forgets, hoping that Dev might see her, feeling that sometimes he really does look at her and understand that she is living an intimate life of immanent revelation right alongside him in every waking breath.

So Marianne has affairs that Dev doesn't know about carried out in various modes of embodied, transcendental, and affective reality. Leon, Patricia, Anusara yoga (the scandal had really wrecked her), Captain Beefheart, agility training with their neighbour's dog Fast Fran, Doug and Tina Cornwall, Leon again (this one was complicated), snowball fights, mosaic funeral portraits, cabinetmaking, Su Lin (she got free wings for a month with this short-lived jaunt), tai chi, the unmaking of thrift store sweaters and remaking of cozy warmers for penguins affected by oil spills, and so on and so forth.

Marianne likes learning new things, some sexual, some practical, and some interpersonal. The way she sees it, community service, environmental activism, and orgasm are all about the same kind of discovery. When she gets real deep in her understanding and sees Dev, really sees him, she knows that Malarkey fulfills something in him that resembles the need she has for the perpetual intimate knowing of things hitherto unknown. Still, she has trouble understanding how he can do it all in his head like that and only rely on her body (less with each successive volume), the sword-fighting club, their domestic space, the gym twice a week when he remembers, and occasional camping trips with Leon to satisfy his physical needs. He eats too but she's pretty sure he takes no real pleasure in it, scarfing down whatever she puts in front of him all the while talking about the newly emergent bio-politics on Pangea II. Coughing on hunks of wasabi as he describes in detail the "reproductive issues arising from the legislative changes finally allowing for full-fledged social participation of humanimal-android spousal units."

Marianne says nothing while Dev, two kernels of soy sauce–splattered rice stuck to his left cheek, explains that Fawn-Pia (the Marianne-doe look-alike) and Trawn 7.3.4 (gold and improved Leon) have not been able to produce viable offspring.

"It just doesn't work, babe, sometimes it just doesn't and it's no one's fault, just, like, the design is messed up. Because, you know, despite the engineering it looks like Trawn shoots blanks. Or at least not the kind of trans-species sperm his model has been designed to manufacture; sperm that should allow for homebred mating so that couples can make their humanimaldroid babies without the need for expensive outsourcing."

Marianne nods, focusing on the taste of the rice, the umami feel of soy sauce and toasted sesame oil on her tongue.

"It could be so fucking amazing, Mari, just imagine, but it's tricky too, I mean, think about it, I've gotta figure out how to make this shit plausible."

Dev is "excited about emergent humanimaldroid sexuality and parenting techniques," he tells Marianne, but still "squeamish about bestiality."

Chapters 4 through 7 of volume 1, laid out in minute detail how the generation of Fawn-Pia's parents, Celeste Parkinson and Stunning Buckungulate, had reproduced through genetic engineering in for-profit black market labs that had threatened the fabric of open-identity exploration on Pangea II.

"Those pseudo-docs, they raked up mad coin with folks trying to make babies. Think about what Celeste and Buckungulate went through for Fawn-Pia. You know, Celeste almost ended up dead without the proper hormones to keep her human womb in the kind of shape it needed to be in for a half-deer baby!"

Marianne starts to clear her plate from the table, gets up without saying anything, while Dev hands her his plate, rushing for his office.

"Hold on, hold on, babe! Let me read that bit to you again, about the first humanimals."

Dev comes back pulling the loose-leaf papers out of their plastic cover and begins reading while Marianne stands at the sink running the water, testing the heat with the back of her left hand, squeezing in the grapefruit-smelling dish soap with her right.[1]

As Dev reads, Marianne holds each dish in her hands,

---

1 Dev's monologue: Though intimate non-sexual human-animal-android companionships were encouraged on Pangea II from its political formation following the environmental and human atrocities of the twenty-first century as the best means to ensure respectful relations among all earth's beings, no one could have predicted the social and genetic upheavals.

It came to pass that some couplets and triplets (quads were rare) forwent the usual course of forming spousal units with their own kind to foster an unregulated conception market that produced Fawn-Pia and a host of other humanimals like her in her age group.

In the beginning Fawn-Pia and the other companion babies were hidden by their parents for their own protection. The very fact of their existence was shared only in intimate subculture caverns, hollows, and sacred clearings carved out by companions wishing to spend time with other couplets and triplets whose intimate lives had been carved into new patterns of kinship by the cross-species bond. But there were just too many of them and the sacred sites were overflowing. Public sightings became more and more common and although Buckungulate and Parkinson had feared the worst for Fawn-Pia, it turned out curiosity rather than fear characterized public perception.

Because of the cross-species love already prominent on Pangea II, the upheaval was fast and mostly non-disruptive (there were a few conservative holdouts but their divisive attitudes could not proliferate on a world that had learned so many lessons from the devastation borne of narratives that separated humankind from the rest of the sensate world).

feeling the ridges of paint on the porcelain, touching gingerly with the pads of her fingers to make sure all the rice starch has been scraped off, rinses briefly, then stacks in the drying rack.

"The trans-species android sperm," Dev tells Marianne, "is a recent invention lobbied for by couplets and triplets who can now be referred to as "spousal units," and therefore deserving of Humanimaldroid Rights to Reproductive Freedom."

Marianne looks at Dev, wondering when the last time was they had a conversation, when the last time was he asked her a question about herself, instead of what seems to her to be this constant "explanating" — going on and on and on about fucking Malarkey. Had he even noticed her tune out when he first said the name "Buckungulate"? She looks back to her dishes, breathing, thinking about her feet touching the earth, noticing her breath stuck in her throat, keeps washing as Dev leans against the door frame, reading emphatically.[2]

Marianne can't help but feel ravaged on the inside by Dev's keen interest in the reproductive lives of his

---

2　Dev's monologue: Though genetic engineering to produce the initial humanimal offspring had been relatively easy to figure out with existing technologies that simply recombined genomes, the machine/biological breeding barrier was harder to figure out. Within one generation the new humanimal offspring had for the most part been able to interbreed with one another and with their human and animal progeni-kin.

Genetics were fluid like that on Pangea II; the government had been lobbied, and the universities received funding for top cybernetics minds (including of course the androids themselves) to work with geneticists to figure out a way to allow for androids to mate in their newly legislated spousal units with humans, animals, and humanimals alike.

inventions while he waffles about their own. Five years they have been trying on and off to conceive, taking breaks after three early miscarriages and dozens of unsuccessful couplings timed perfectly within the days of prime fertility. But Marianne is nearing forty now, nearing it so close she has to hold her toes back to keep from touching it, knowing all the while the waters will rise and there she'll be swimming in the tidal changes of her body, inched past her reproductive years. Although now of "advanced maternal age," medical tests confirm that her reproductive system is in good standing, with functioning ovaries, viable eggs, and a well-lined uterus. Dev's tests, according to him, indicate "a good count of swimmers in his spunk."

"'Kay, thanks for dinner, babe, I got an idea I want to figure out," Dev says as Marianne puts the last dish in the rack. He walks out of the kitchen, back to his den, sits down at his desk, and plugs his earbuds in. Marianne can see his back from the kitchen sink. She walks slowly to the dish-towel hanging on the stove and dries her hands. Flicks off the lamp over the kitchen sink, looking at her reflection in the dark window, past her sad-looking eyes to the outside world where she can just make out the silhouette of the pear tree in the twilight. She rests her dish-wrinkled hands on her lower abdomen, feeling the singularness of herself, sensing a quiet screaming.

Marianne pictures a coup taking place in her body — instead of travelling diligently down her fallopian tubes only during ovulation, Marianne's eggs travel from her ovaries while she sleeps and set up a big messy nest in her mind. She can think of nothing but these soldier eggs intent on mobilizing every resource to draw forth Dev's minuscule contribution for them to start developing into babies.

During fertile days she finds herself ordering crotchless panties online and stuffing herself into the slinkiest of dresses, everything about her just a bit more slutty — makeup rouging her face, a sway to her hips that other times isn't there.

Each coming of blood marks another devastation. She returns temporarily to a state of calm and feels frightened of the urges within herself that do not seem of herself at all.

⁓

Dev had been clear he didn't want to get back on the roller coaster of her cycle before Malarkey had come to completion, pulling out, slipping a condom on, or claiming headaches. It was too hard on their emotional lives, he had said the last time she brought it up, going on a tirade that had sent Marianne into the latest fugue of silence that Dev seemed not to have noticed. She went over it again in her head.

"It's all so typical — all these women now, so intent on meaningful lives putting things off while the whole time their clocks are ticking and then clamouring desperately for uterine fulfillment to add more babies to an already overpopulated world. It's boring, so unlike the possibilities for procreation available on Pangea II!"

Marianne had put a lot of years into Dev LaRue. Sure, he was sometimes an asshole unwilling to sway very far from his own beliefs about things, unable to connect with his emotional being, but he was also the man she had made her life with, intertwined, familiar, an anchor in her relations with the world. She had been agitated since Dev had shared his social analysis of her suffering, ridiculing her for the commonplace feelings of women "her age." It was humiliating.

For weeks she fumed and sputtered, biting at her nails, going around things in her head convinced of what she'd suspected all along—that his uncertainties and self-interest would rob her of a motherhood she had once waffled about wanting, but that was now the thing she desired most to make real.

~

Marianne began to read blogs written by other "predictable" women who had waited to become mothers and were now pressed by time—women with flourishing creative, intellectual, and personal lives in relationships with men reluctant to become fathers. She read descriptions of supercharged uteruses, spitfire ovaries, hormonal overlords, and accusations of spermjacking by the men who claimed to love them.

Marianne decided to be as "typical" as possible for a woman her age. She reread *Eat, Pray, Love*, and after closing the last page, she quit her design job for *Real Yoga Magazine* and made plans to leave for three months to figure out how she wanted to be when she came back, or if she wanted to come back at all.

Inspired by Elizabeth Gilbert but wanting to design her own personalized journey of discovery, she decided to go first to an ashram in India, then for a trek in Nepal. Her final month was set for Japan where she was registered for a three-week immersion course in Japanese cookery.

To India she went solo, hoping for a spiritual revelation that would help her pick a path forward. From there she travelled north by train to meet the Cornwalls in Katmandu. Doug and Tina trekked in Nepal every couple of years. They had contacts there they now called friends and porters they trusted to carry their high-end gear. This year they had invited Marianne to join them after India knowing she needed to get away for a while, rethink things with Dev, and make decisions about what her life was going to look like.

A month in India had given her no resolution, only a bad case of food poisoning and a deeper understanding that love was an attachment that would cause her suffering whichever way she went forward. She could stay and remain childless, loving Dev unconditionally for the selfish asshole that he sometimes was, do the baby thing on her own, or renounce earthly desires, take vows of celibacy, and give herself over to spiritual pursuits and daily life in an ashram (Marianne was into firm choices and ultimatums, could not live a life suspended in ambiguity).

There were movies and other kinds of memoirs and support groups now for modern single moms doing the baby thing, women like her who had not found the man they were looking for or had found the man they were looking for and it hadn't worked out the way they had planned. Or women who weren't interested in men at all and just wanted to have a baby on their own. They brought up sperm-donor babies and blogged about it, letting other solo moms know about the challenges but also the heartfelt joys of doing it on their own (easier, some said, than having to worry about the relationship on top of the mothering). The Cornwalls said they would help, even offered up the sperm for old times' sake, take a friendly interest in the baby's life, but not in any implicated way. They had their own adolescent children already and appreciated the freedom now to get away on their own while their daughters worked at summer camps. Marianne knew she wasn't ready to stay at the ashram long term. Her sexual interests were not quite suited to permanent celibacy.

So Marianne set off to the Kanchenjunga base camp with the Cornwalls, still hoping that resolution would find its

way to her, that she'd know for sure one way or the other.
She went up with a pious and open heart and although she
had told herself she wouldn't, that she needed to redirect
her desires toward spiritual understanding, she and the
Cornwalls got up to their old tricks on the way back down.
The heights had thrilled them all, their bodies rushing with
habits of daily physical exertion that looped their minds into
immediacies of doing, plus they had reasoned it was lighter
to carry one rather than two tents on the trip (the Cornwalls
felt it important for an authentic experience that they carry
as much of their own gear as possible, not putting too much
of a load on the porters' backs who they worried they might
be taking advantage of because of their Western privilege).

The Cornwalls wanted to fuck Marianne out of her
stupor, they said, and while they did she was free of her
grief for a while, longing for their naked heat that smelled
of musky yak milk and tasted of thin air as their days of
constant motion turned into nights of sweaty drinking,
rocking, tasting, fusing on steep and rocky slopes.

The randiness was still with her after the Cornwalls flew
back and Dev surprised her at the guesthouse on her last
night in Katmandu. He missed her, he said, and wanted to
take her to visit some of the sites he'd learned about during
research on Nepalese ritualistic swords for a sequence he
was writing into Malarkey. Marianne (despite the fact that
Dev had a selfish side project as an explanation for following
her) felt smitten by the romance of his coming for her all the

way across seas and continents. She carried the fervour of the Cornwalls' ministrations into the peeling plaster walls of the guesthouse, and Dev, outside his regular routines of home life responded with an enthusiasm she hadn't seen in him since the advent of Malarkey. They stayed on for weeks, researching, eating, wandering, and rediscovering each other's strangely adaptive bodies.

In Katmandu Marianne learned from Dev that there had been some technological developments on Pangea II that he had not anticipated.

"Fawn-Pia," Dev proclaimed while stuffing mouthfuls of richly pungent dal bhat into his mouth with his fingers, "has still not been able to conceive Trawn 7.3.4's baby through direct sperm-to-ovule contact, but they have been able to extract Fawn-Pia's gametes and fuse them with equivalent information from Trawn 7.3.4's basic personality subroutines to create viable embryos that they are planning to implant both in Fawn-Pia's uterus, and also, get this, in Trawn 7.3.4's newly activated robotowomb!"

Dev looked at Marianne in a way that made her think he was seeing her. He told her that in chronicling Fawn-Pia and Trawn 7.3.4's reproductive challenges he had overlooked the fact that "the Trawn 7.3.4 unit came with the option of expressing male, female, or hermaphroditic sexual characteristics."

Reaching for Marianne's hand he said, "Although the robotowomb is at this point only theoretically able to carry a cyborg fetus to full term, programming and generating the necessary information for it to carry out its own growth and development, I believe that under the guidance of regular input from medico-engineers Trawn 7.3.4 will be successful in gestating at least one of the embryos to birth.

"Fawn-Pia's chances I'm still somewhat uncertain about. After all there's so much to be learned about how these new humanimaldroid possibilities might work."

～

Marianne Thickenson's baby is a little odd looking with that gold skin and huge deer-like eyes. It won't be until he's older though that people will notice the leaping. And only a few will ever see the perky white tail he'll keep tucked close under tight-fitting briefs, saved only for the most intimate of encounters.

The baby is difficult and demanding. He rearranges Marianne in ways she had never considered. He is not at all what she was led to believe based on all the cards she received about the joys and wonders of motherhood. He is not like those calm, sleeping caricatures all haloed in light, radiating joy and completion, but rather a yelping, suckling thing that expunges fluids everywhere and makes her body leaky and soft.

Marianne has very strong feelings toward the baby.

The feelings pull at her to act with an intensity of love that clamps and pulsates her whole being. She learns as she cares for the baby that a spirit bound to flesh suffers as it arrives in this world. Marianne wants to ease its suffering and gives most of herself to do this. Sometimes she feels that in all this giving she will disappear. Parts of her do in fact disappear, while unintended ones emerge.

The baby grows into its own person as Marianne grows into her own person. That is what motherhood is, thinks Marianne, growing into your own person alongside an unpredictable being that is of the world and of you and therefore sacred. Sacredness is not a simple thing so there are a lot of prostrations involved. The body gets sore and tired. Meanwhile the spirit reveals itself in quiet moments to have been reunited with part of its universal self— connected through time to all the mothers before and all those that will come after. Marianne is in the world as a continuation of her lineage instead of just as herself. Although she is no longer free in time to exercise her wants and flow her mind into everything through the force of her own curiosity and recklessness, she is free from the constraint of always having to pursue herself and this opens up new ways of embodied being. There is suffering and remarkability in all of it.

Sleeplessness wrecks Marianne for the first year of the baby's life. Dev is awkward about caring for the baby. He always gives it back to Marianne because it confuses him.

He thinks he might domesticate himself to it by writing it into Malarkey. Marianne rips the pages out when he shows them to her because Dev's rendition of the baby is monstrous. A beetle-like thing that learns through a series of developmentally timed subroutines how not to devour the world. Chemical inoculants injected into its caregivers to make them want to care for it.

The baby has satisfied a need for full attention that Marianne was always looking for in relationships with men. Full attention that Dev found stifling. The endless, brutal nurturing that he wanted to turn on only when he needed it, thinking somehow Marianne could turn it off when he was occupied with other things.

Here she is beholden to a wriggly, vibrant little thing that can always take more than she can give, wanting so much of her. What a ruse that she thought this feeling had been meant for a man! With so much of the baby to occupy her mind, Dev's lack of love becomes less personal, or at least stops hurting in the ways it used to. Marianne sees that Dev is unravelling in the absence of her attention. He grows resentful of her and the baby, making quips at them when they cuddle on the couch, refusing to help with waking and feeding and the fluids that leak everywhere. Marianne comes to see him as a foreign world, crashing into the world she and the baby occupy, unhinging them with his needs.

They try for a while, thinking things will change, get easier, and at first Marianne believes that even though Dev seems unable to love the baby, he might learn. She recounts wonderful things about the baby, trying to encourage Dev's interest, but most of the time he does not respond. Still, she feels she might need Dev around for practical reasons, like allowing her to shower once in a while, or picking things up at the grocery. Small things that he sometimes does for her "as a favour."

Marianne thinks maybe she does not need Dev in particular, just someone who can give her a break once in a while, someone who might even love the baby without resenting it. Dev begins to disappear more fully into Malarkey, so much so that more and more he begins to confuse his imaginary and domestic worlds. Until one day Marianne goes into his room and finds what seems like an incomplete manuscript for volume 7. She calls around to Leon and to Dev's mother in Lac La Hache, but no one has heard from Dev in days. None of his things are missing, all of the swords stashed neatly in their cases. It will be two weeks before she rereads the pages he left behind and fully understands that Dev found a way to write himself in.

She sees him there as he had always wished to be seen, engaged in an epic sword fight with Trawn 7.3.4 as Fawn-Pia nurses the most magnificent creature in her arms.

"So this is what you were going for?" she asks the Dev on the page, feeling like she has finally understood him in a way she was not able to when he was his fleshy self, living and breathing in her home alongside her. Dev is alive in Malarkey in a way he seemed unable to be in real life. Marianne closes the book and puts it away to give to the baby later, when he becomes curious about his father.

Family Sketches

I

My father had a hero leg and was strong and bold, jumping higher than the other fathers, running faster. We were fortunate to have him, valued as he was in the community for his odd feats of physical prowess.

Because our father had a hero leg, but none of us daughters were imparted with his gift, we sometimes became nervous. The townsfolk would often look at us crossways, as though they were expecting something. We shuffled past them, dipping our heads and bowing our shoulders slightly so that they would not be threatened by our awkwardness.

Our father was proud of us, even though he sometimes said we were useless. For instance, once I overheard him tell the pharmacist that we were good girls at heart, quick-witted, yet physically unsuccessful.

One of my sisters claims father's hero leg was a trade-off; that in exchange for all that glory he had to agree to some force or other not to pass anything spectacular on to his daughters so as not to garner too much good fortune in one family. Some of us, but not the trade-off sister, still think the best of father, and we support him in his feats, even though we are often unhelpful.

2

These are my sisters' friends; they are all very fast, hanging on to this or that bit of word to make them move faster! They swing about the world, barely touching the ground, eating sprigs of rosemary as they pass by to keep their breath fresh and help them speak faster.

My sisters' friends are busy, look at them go about their tasks! They chart the movement of planets, write books on the lives of saints and cane toads, recite poetry in fifteen languages (at least two of them oral, and therefore only transmissible as spoken word), make love with glorious beings, villains, and regular folk, and sleep, always soundly, when the time is right.

I do not trust my sisters' friends, but I love them. I love the way their hair looks like glass because of the speeds at which they travel, stunning me with the sheen of light reflecting into myriad colours whenever they pass by.

If I could, I would be one of my sisters' friends, but

because I am their sister I can only look on, sometimes able to build up enough speed to make a small thatch village and then destroy it, along with the inhabitants, and other times able to just sit quietly amongst the high-pitched sound of women talking, making tiny words that explode into tiny worlds I then inhabit.

3

My father has blue eyes the colour of this morning's sky over the Gorge Waterway. His eyes are the blue of forget-me-nots washed over in the sun's white light.

My mother's eyes are not light, not light at all but dark, somewhere between green and brown where you dig a shovel into grass and turn the dirt over.

These days my mother wears glasses that darken when exposed to direct sunlight. It is very distracting when it happens indoors, sitting across from each other at breakfast, when suddenly she turns, the light obfuscating, rather than revealing her intentions.

4

My sister knows how to fall in love; she tells me it is easy.

"You sit and focus on your lover's teeth," she says.

"Watch closely; when you look away again, you'll notice that you did not notice as the world went by."

I look at my lover's teeth and become distracted by a buildup of plaque near the gum line, a slight odour of sourness and flecks of something green lodged in his smile, fissures that might turn into cracks as he ages.

"Is this love then?" I ask my sister, but she tells me that this is a corruption of love.

For weeks, in order to remedy this corruption I think only of teeth, use any medium I can think of to make them: stones, sticks, paper, plastic cartons, bits of coloured glass, shrivelled carrots, and broccoli stems. I collect shells at the beach and fashion them into teeth beads that I wear around my neck to assure myself that I am a medium for the most precious kind of love. In honour of my lover I scratch fissures into the teeth beads, lodge bits of seaweed into the spaces between them, dip them in soups but do not deign to clean them so that an awkward smell is always coming from them, even in the freshest air of spring.

"I am so much in love," I tell the folks at the office who talk about the new kinds of magnets they've found to fasten to their metallic desks that have photos of their children printed on them doing things they think are funny.

I am asked not to wear my teeth beads to work because of their unsightliness and odour, and I suspect it is because Janet, across from me, is jealous of my profound unfolding. To honour the deepness of the love that I am living, I sew a plastic zip-locked bag into the hemline of my office skirts where I keep the teeth hidden as I undertake my daily tasks of tapping keys and moving papers from one place to another.

Even though I am being vigilant in attention to my lover's teeth I notice that the world continues to go by, despite my best efforts. There is evidence of this everywhere, but most particularly in the silent air that hangs between the triad of our love: his teeth, my teeth, secret effigies of my love for him tucked in the hemline of my skirts.

The problem occurs in nakedness when there are only his teeth, and mine, and a supposed proposition of timelessness. Words and thoughts dwell within the forests of our teeth but they seem such different worlds. The teeth across the room are talking to me, how plain their happiness!

He is saying something about my standards of measurement. Teeth, teeth, teeth, so many teeth for tasting, spitting, talking, sucking, biting, and tearing bits of food from bone.

My mother says that my sister is more adept at loving. She says it is because of our natures. Instead of love I am assigned qualities of purposefulness and rigour.

5

My mother has a tall order of gifts to fill for the oncoming season, but instead of giving gifts she'll give her blood to the secret saints she keeps hidden in the back closet.

She built a fake wall in the back of that back closet so that we wouldn't know her saints were there. But I heard her hammering in the night, I saw her carry stones into the dark, I felt the wind rush out when the saints spoke words she thought only she could hear.

A Family Story

I was looking for my mother's porcelain cup, but she had hidden it from me. She knew I would come by looking, knew also that father would forget not to give it over if I was around asking, so she hid it somewhere and wrote a secret note that would not arrive until she died.

It has never been clear why mother hid the cup, or why she entrusted the secret note to father, who was sure to forget, or die before she did.

Every once in a while I still go around to their old place, where no one lives now since my sisters and I cannot agree on who should live there. I sneak in through the back window because the eldest sister has the key that she keeps locked in her lawyer's office downtown. She tried to hire a security guard once, to keep me out of the place, but I simply started to suck him off and then sleep with him, even bringing him around to dinner once for some family affair. After that she gave up, since she knew me well enough to know I'd find my way in somehow.

Mother's porcelain cup is not a rarity. There are thousands of others like it, aside from the tiny chip in the base where I once clipped it against the dish rack after the morning dishes. Mother scowled then, but later on was happy to have some peculiarity that set her cup apart from all the other cups in the set, which were also hers, but without affection or mythological import.

The other porcelain cups had narrative, but not meaning: they came in the mail just after the birth of the third daughter, when father's mother decided it was high time they acknowledge the union, even if it was a sinful one. But mother never liked those cups, they were just a burden to her, how she had nowhere to put them that would do them justice and no one to serve tea to, since the local folk only drank coffee, and only in bowl-sized cups with thick rims, cups you could wrap your hands around to keep warm in the dim of winter.

The porcelain cups were in the morning dishes because mother, in an unusual act of charity, had allowed us to drink our milk from them the night before. We were always begging her to be allowed to touch them, for a sip or two of water, being as careful as we were with the tiny spring chicks, whose necks could snap so quickly.

Mother had allowed us, and we had been so proud! She even showed us how to tip the pinky out, our grubby fingers daintily curved, following the contours of the cups.

We had slept afterwards, each one of us with our own set
of dreams, our own rituals for the turning of wakefulness
to slumber.

I woke early, as I always did, but on that day earlier, in
order to fondle the cups, clean them up, shine them, before
mother came watching. I chipped the one and tried to hide
it under the others so mother wouldn't know it was me, but
when she came into the kitchen and looked at the stacked
cups, she scowled at me, knowing.

After that, mother used the cup daily, used it for coffee
or rum, sometimes wine or Grand Marnier. She used it for
her own purposes, and in so doing made it hers. I was still
not allowed to touch it because mother said she did not
want it broken any further.

Perhaps mother hid the cup because she did not want
me to take her on, to take her up, to become like the parts
of her that she struggled daily to live with—a little chip
where shame flourished, always threatening to crack right
through the veneer. Yet special too, the chip, allowing for
a malleability of purpose unimaginable with those other
perfect cups meant to invite people into a space mother did
not know how to hold. If you held the chip up to your lip
while sipping, anyone looking on would see only the beauty
of the cup, not knowing the tender and dangerous feel of
the chip that could cut through your lip if you pressed it a
certain way.

Mom's Online Dating Profile

Camilla's mother had talked about finding a soulmate a lot in her life. Talked about it startlingly soon after Camilla's father had passed away, talked about it right up until her own unexpected death at seventy-four.

Just a month before her accident, she'd talked to Camilla about how since her husband had been dead over a year now, she felt she could begin to start looking again. After fifty years with the same man! She told Camilla that although she had loved him, it had been a long time since anything resembling passion had passed between them. Anything resembling recognition, really, either. They got by. They took care of each other in the ways they knew how, but he had not been interested in any kind of emotional connection. And Camilla's mother had long ago stopped listening when he got on about whatever had caught his fancy on television. So they talked about groceries and dinner, things needing done around the house. She would relay information about the grandkids to him, since he would never be the one to call the kids directly. He was happy to hear though, always happy to hear about how the kids and grandkids were getting on.

"I still know he's out there somewhere," was what her mother had said. "Freda said a year is long enough to tastefully start looking again." And Camilla had felt angry, like her mother was betraying her father somehow, like the fifty years meant nothing somehow if it only took one year to be ready to move on, holding her tongue about relying on Freda as a barometer for tastefulness.

"What do you mean, mom? Like you really think you will meet someone now, in your mid-seventies? And what would you do with them? Really?"

"It isn't like that, Cammie, not all about sex the way it is for young people. I'm talking about really seeing one another. I may look old to you on the outside, but I'm still me on the inside, same as I've always been. Well, it doesn't matter; you aren't interested in knowing what I really mean. No one is. No one ever is except Freda. She, at least, doesn't judge me."

Fucking Freda again, thought Camilla, yes of course Freda is the only person in the world you actually like! Well, it's not like you listen to anything I say or think, but.... Okay, Camilla, get a hold of yourself, she's not going to change now. Try to listen to her for god's sake. "I'm not judging you, mom, I'm just surprised. I didn't know you were still interested. I mean, you used to talk about it all the time during the rough patches with dad, I guess, but I haven't heard you mention it in a while. I thought you and dad had figured it out."

"Well, we did. In the ways we did. And got on fine with each other in the end, maybe because we both got tired, who knows. But the way I see it, him dying first, well. It's not that I mean to say it's a gift or anything, lord knows, but it gives me certain freedoms to think about my life in a different way."

"Okay mom, I want you to be happy. I just want you to be careful too." Camilla did want her mom to be happy. She also worried that her mom would get caught up in things that Camilla would end up having to deal with in one way or another. She'd gotten used to her mother being the way she was with her father, and then the last year, figuring it out with her to make sure she had the things she needed now that dad was gone, but this would change things again, if there were someone else. Well, but how likely was it? Where was she going to meet this person anyway?

"I didn't want to tell you before now because I knew you would think it was too soon after dad passing, but Freda helped me set up a profile a few months ago. It was kind of fun. We took some classy pictures. You know how Freda is with her camera. Her Instagram has a lot of followers. Mostly pictures of her grandkids, you know, but she knows about light and even had me take some shots out at the park. I was embarrassed! Oh, but we laughed a lot. We always do. People looked. You don't usually see a seventy-four-year-old woman doing a classy photo shoot in the park! Ha! Well, the ducks didn't seem fazed. Even got me feeding them in a few shots. I had to make sure my dress wasn't dragging in the duck poo."

"Are you serious, mom? Online dating? You barely know how to email! And there are a lot of creeps out there. I mean, a lot! You can't just trust that people are who they say they are."

"Oh, Cammie, you're always worried about everything. I'm not stupid. Freda is helping me screen people. She knows all about the internet."

"Mom, this is serious; it could be dangerous. Can't you just meet men at the seniors' centre or something, if you feel like you have to? Do you have a plan, at least, for how you'll meet up with people? It's just that you're vulnerable, mom, and people could take advantage of you. I don't want to see you get hurt."

"Do you have to make everything so un-fun? I wish I hadn't told you. I'm not your kid; I'm your mom. I'll do as I please and it's none of your business."

Camilla knew she was too frustrated to keep at this. That she'd have to change the subject and come back to this later, because now they were both on the defence and neither was listening to the other. Why did there always have to be these power struggles? This suspicion between them? Like they had to be policing each other or something? Why couldn't they just listen to each other like she did with her girlfriends and mom did with Freda? She could talk with Freda like a person, hell, often had to go that route to get something across to her mother. She'd probably have to do that now, talk to Freda. To make sure.

"Okay, mom, I don't want to talk about this anymore. But I would like to see the photos, that Freda took?"

"Oh, yes, you can see those; I'm quite proud of them, really. I mean, I look old. But I am old, even if I don't feel like it on the inside, so may as well not try to pretend I still look as good as you do—but Freda did a good job, I think, with my angles and all that. But I'm not showing you my profile, so don't ask. That's private."

Camilla had gone home after that conversation, not knowing then that this would be one of the last they would have that wasn't about groceries, appointments, or what the kids were up to at school. She thought on the drive home about how it made her uncomfortable to think about mom still looking for a man who really saw her, after all this time, and how she was just like her mother, still pining after something despite what she had. But what she had wasn't worth pining over; she already had it. And it was so dull most of the time. Why had she thought this life was something worth swooning over at one time? Well, it wasn't this life, not really; this wasn't what she'd imagined. This was just an updated version of her mom and dad's life, wasn't it? No shag carpet, but how different were her and Noel's roles, really? They had talked about things being different, "equitable," was how Noel had put it. He had studied some feminist theory in his poli-sci classes, hadn't he? Could read novels written by women, sometimes. Had flirted with bisexuality in undergrad, but decided cock wasn't for him, other than his own. They'd even discussed polyamory at some point, hadn't they? God, what a lot of work that would be! Camilla couldn't imagine. No, when she imagined something else now, it was mostly quiet gazing into someone's eyes. Lying there, in stillness, without feeling you had to look away for some reason. Those eyes being benevolent or something, deep too, like a still, glacial lake. She didn't want to be touched, or have to do any touching. She just wanted to lie there, looking, and then fall asleep without having to do anything else. Without feeling she needed to. Without feeling there were things that had to be said, or worked through, to get to a place of seeing each other. And it wasn't something ongoing, either; it was just like some kind of refuge she could go to when she needed to, and then leave without having to explain why. A refuge that might exist, kind of like dragons might exist, somewhere, and there might be some way to get to that world if we knew how. Like her daughter had said to her the other night before bed, making a wish on a star outside the window. A wish she didn't want to be secret, that she could go to another world, with her mom, on another planet.

Mulling things over in her head that night—tracing over the conversation with mom, how it hadn't gone the way either of them wanted, leaving them feeling suspicious of each other rather than in it together, and then touching on the closeness she felt with her daughter now—Camilla felt a sort of sadness that she couldn't remember wanting to be with her mom that much. Had she? Wanted that at some point as a child? Had her mom ever had enough time to give her that she would have listened to Camilla's dreams? It was sad we couldn't remember those years when our mothers gave so much to us, thought Camilla. She knows her mother breastfed her, and got her through infancy, and there are photos of them cuddling, from back then. Of her mom looking at her unguarded, love in her eyes, even looking at the person behind the camera that way, Camilla's father. So she had loved him too, at some point. Maybe that's what this is all about, really, thought Camilla, wanting to be loved like that again, in all our helplessness, before we had the words to turn the emotions into something else. A body memory of that? Then she thought about babies who didn't have that time with their mothers, and did they feel that too, or just the absence of it? Or maybe someone else had given it to them? Or not? And then Camilla didn't want to think about it anymore. She still had to figure out how to approach the online dating profile with Freda in

such a way that Freda would get it and wouldn't just run
and tell her mom Camilla was trying to control things
through her again.

~⌒~

Two years after her mother's death Camilla found herself
thinking about that online dating profile. Remembering
how she had worried so much in that month between
finding out her mom was online dating and her mom's
death. And had it been warranted? She wishes now she
had known she had such little time left with her mom,
that she had supported her better somehow, rather than
worrying about what might happen. Still, she wasn't sure,
couldn't shake a niggling feeling that there was a link
between mom's dating profile and her death, a link she
wasn't seeing.

Camilla hadn't gotten a chance to talk to Freda about it
before mom died, and then, living through the shock and
the grief, she had put it out of her mind. She wanted to ask
Freda about it now, she just didn't know how to bring it
up since Freda was still so very, very upset about Marlise.

Not that Freda being upset was out of the ordinary —
Freda and Marlise had been so close, but it did seem to
Camilla that Freda was torn up about something beyond
the loss of her friend. Camilla had seen that at the memorial for the second anniversary of mom's death last week.

She hadn't seen Freda since the year before—when things had still felt so raw for her that she wasn't so much paying attention to what Freda was feeling. She'd meant to reach out to Freda since then, but hadn't. Had sent a few emails, but it was hard to tell over email how people were feeling. At this recent memorial though, Freda had been a mess! Camilla had almost been embarrassed.

Camilla was thinking about the research she had done about seniors' dating sites before mom had died, looking to see if she could dig anything up about scams, or frauds, and how different sites went about security protocols. She had bookmarked some pages to send to mom with articles about protecting yourself online. She hadn't realized there were so many seniors' dating sites out there! She had thought it might be easy to set up a fake account and find out what her mom was up to that way, but she'd first have to find out which site her mom was using, and then probably have to get one of her friends' dads, who her mom didn't know, to set up a fake profile so she could online spy on her mom's dating profile to make sure her mom was safe. It was going to take a lot of work. She'd sent out a few emails to her girlfriends, explaining the situation, but none of them had gotten back with a definite yes about a dad willing to help her out with this. She didn't have the energy to make up her own fake profile. She liked the idea of that, imagining what kind of man her mom might go for, but faking an identity, finding photos to go with that, maybe having to do some fake correspondence. Well, wouldn't she then be committing fraud on her mom? Shit. It was all so complicated. Better just to get one of her friends' dads to do it, have a peek, make sure her mom wasn't putting herself out there online in ways that would attract creeps. You know, saying things like "recently widowed," or making it seem like she had a lot of money someone could get their hands on. She had some, not a lot, but enough that someone could get something if they managed to trick her into it with her naive impressions about love.

Camilla was thinking about how she never had seen those photos of mom that Freda took, and that she would like to. She was also thinking about Freda — how she should really be checking in on her more often. Camilla wondered if Freda still felt guilty about mom's fall. Not that it had been her fault, but they had been drinking together, Freda and mom, drinking too much, probably. Freda had been the one to find her in the morning. Had spent the night at mom's place because they had drank too much white wine for Freda to drive home. Hadn't even heard mom call out, or the vase breaking — that godawful thing Camilla had given her in the '90s that mom had held on to, still the same dried grasses that she brought out and dusted once a year in springtime. Shards of glass everywhere, and the terracotta tiles. It hadn't been pretty.

Camilla still remembers seeing the blood on the dried grass, how sad she felt about that. How she knew mom would have been upset about the mess she had caused, the way she had so much hated messes. Freda had been frantic when she'd called Camilla.

"God, oh god, Cammie! I don't know what to do. You have to get over here now! Now, Cammie, to your mom's place. My god! Oh Marlise, oh god..."

"Freda, Freda? What is it, what's happened?" Camilla had said something like that. Trying to get Freda to talk, to tell her what had happened. Her heart up in her throat, knowing it was something bad. Freda had been sobbing hard, then whimpering and snivelling. Like a hurt dog? No, something else, something bone-chilling, horrific even. Camilla's neck hairs went up. She grabbed her keys, cell phone in hand, and ran out the door in her nightgown, the sexy one she'd worn the night before, for her and Noel's once-a-week date night. She'd kept it on while they...

"Maarliiissse! Huh-huh-huh. Sweetie, ohh, Marlise..." And Freda had trailed off, hanging up before Camilla could press her for more information.

But there it was. Her mother was dead on the floor at the bottom of her stairs. Gruesomely dead. Cuts and bruises all over her beautiful crepe paper skin, the smooth age-spot-freckled light brown skin on Marlise's hands that Camilla's daughter loved to pet while grandma read stories to her, making up characters that weren't even in the book. How

Camilla's little girl loved that, the way grandma changed the story every time. Not Camilla, or Noel, no, they had to read it the same way each time, or she'd make them stop, do it over again.

Camilla stood there, half naked, looking at her mom's bent body, the blood, the cuts on Freda's hands and legs bleeding too. Freda holding her most beloved friend in her strong arms and weeping. And Camilla had laughed, because it all seemed so absurd, so outside the scope of their regular lives. Her and Freda and mom, three almost naked women and all that blood. It was absurd. Then something clicked in her. The laugh buried itself in her chest, becoming a gasp, and then a heave. Camilla had bent over heaving, and that voice, the one that came to her sometimes when she was having to deal with her mother, that voice came through and said to her, "Calm down, honey; you're going to have to calm down. You. Are. Going. To. Have. To. Dealwiththis. Deal with this." Yes, of course. Deal with this. If nothing else, Camilla knew how to deal with things. It was plain. Something was going to have to be done. Mom was dead, clearly dead, and Freda was bleeding all over the place. Freda.

It got blurry from there. Smudged out. How things progressed. But Camilla could pan back to that first absurd snapshot, visiting it again and again in her mind as though it were a painting she liked to stare at in a fine art museum somewhere, rendered by a surrealist who liked to mangle the female form, mess up the cues of ordinary life, for some reason. A painting one of her university roommates might have bought an oversized poster of at those sales they used to have at the beginning of the year for kids just away from home for the first time to buy to decorate the crappy rooms they rented that the landlords never painted between tenants.

Camilla would think of her mom's death like that for a long time, as a surrealist painting, a surrealist painting made into a cheap oversized poster hanging on a chemistry student's dingy wall. She would feel herself almost naked looking at it, the satiny feel of her sexy nightgown and the way it felt when it had slid around on her skin the night before her mother's death, between her and her husband's bodies.

Camilla had phoned 911. Freda had not thought to do that. They had taken Freda to hospital for the wounds, and given her something to sedate her. Camilla had called Noel; he had come after finding someone to take the kids. She didn't remember who. He went onto Camilla's Facebook and sent a message to Freda's daughter Carmen, who lived in the interior somewhere, a ranch or something? He gave her his cell number and she called within the hour. She would come, but it was a twelve-hour drive. It would take some time for her to get there. Freda was sedated so it would be okay that Carmen couldn't get there right away. Noel had said something like that.

It was hard to believe that two years had passed already. Camilla still looked at the painting-poster of her mother's death in her mind sometimes, but not as often. She mostly remembered other things about her mother's life. The ways they had never understood each other, or seen each other as women, but loved each other nonetheless, and how so many of her own habits and gestures were her mother's habits and gestures. Ones she didn't like, mostly, but had been learning to forgive herself for since her mother's death, because she was learning to forgive her mother for all the things she had wished her mother had been that she hadn't been.

So Camilla was surprised at how torn up Freda was still. Certainly, having been the one who found mom would have been a shock. And Freda had maybe still been drunk when she had found her. But that might have helped too, maybe? Or not; it hadn't seemed to. And they had been drinking together, so maybe it was that Freda couldn't forgive herself. Camilla had been working on forgiveness. She wanted Freda to forgive herself. She thought mom would have wanted that too.

Camilla decided to give Freda a call to see if there was anything she could do to help Freda get over what had happened. But first, she thought she'd message Carmen to see if Carmen had anything to share that could help her understand where Freda was at with things. When Camilla brought up Messenger, Carmen was online so they had a chat.

Saw Freda the other day, at mom's memorial. She was pretty distraught. I'm worried about her.

Yah she told me it was Marlises memorial two years, god, how r u doin?

Better, okay. I miss her tonnes, but better. The kids are still really sad. When they remember. Tessa dreams about her a lot.

Yah, she was a good gramma loved those kids.

So I'm wondering about Freda. Is she ok?

I dunno she's Freda right sometimes she seems giddy like and other times anxious maybe snappish like defensive or sad I dont see her much, bein out here once a year, twice? she wont come out too buggy or snowy too far ya know?

I've never been out that way, but yes, it seems far. When was the last time you talked with her.

Every Sunday we Facetime with the kids she eats that up, them too but yah, we dont say much those calls kids r always talking bout their stuff know what I mean? I guess a month, maybe since she and I talked fer real she seemed ok said she was spending time with a "gentleman!" said maybe next time we were up we could meet him from out of town she said someone we wouldn't know

Okay, wonder who that could be? Well good for her. She just seemed a bit strange. You know?

K I'll call her to check but if you wouldnt mind taking her for coffee or somethin checking in on her? If yer worried let me know?

Sure, I will Carmen, I'll let you know. Give me a shout next time you're up. We got a trampoline last summer. Kids could come over and play.

K, sounds good ttfn.

It hadn't given Camilla much, but it had given her a place to start. It didn't seem like Freda was depressed exactly, mourning all the time still, but it sounded like something was up with the way she was up and down all the time. Poor Freda. It must have been hard on her. And Carmen not around much. Freda was so social though; she had always been in all those groups, still was, Camilla was pretty sure. Camilla really should have been checking in on her more these past few years, it's just that it took Camilla a good year to get back on her own feet, and life had still been so busy. Still though, it wasn't right, after all Freda had been like an aunt to Camilla growing up. Something like an aunt— though Camilla had resented her sometimes for being so close to mom, always being the one mom turned to, instead of turning to Camilla. Camilla would have liked that some- times. Not the way mom used to do it though, those years Freda was gone and things weren't good with dad. The way she would talk about him and Camilla always felt she had to stand up for him, wanting mom to see his side of things too, and then mom would fly off the handle at her, saying why did she bother, Camilla always picked his side anyway.

Camilla remembers wondering why there always had to be sides. She hadn't understood then, but she understood now how that happened in a relationship. That competition. Dad never said things like that, about mom behind her back; he just said the mean things he had to say right to mom's face, then he'd brood for a bit, muttering under his breath all the time for days, then never mentioning it again, going back to cracking jokes. Mom though, on and on she'd go, picking apart at him, all his faults. The way Camilla did now with Noel sometimes. In her mind if not out loud. Camilla remembers wishing Freda were around then to be a listening ear for her mother. Maybe Freda didn't care hearing those things, but he was Camilla's dad and it bothered her to hear them. She had her own things she hated him for; she didn't need to know the things mom hated him for too. It was usually then, those times, that mom would talk about wanting to leave and find another man. Someone she could talk to about things, someone who was interested in doing the work with her instead of always just being the same old stubborn, boring, angry man all the time. And Camilla remembers wondering, Why don't you then? Why don't you just go? She never said that to mom, she didn't really want her to go, but she thought if mom did go, she'd stay with dad because he would seem so sad otherwise.

"Freda? Hey Freda, it's me, Camilla. How are you doing? What's that? Sorry, you're cutting out there."

"Hello? Hello? Cammie? That you, Cammie?"

"Yes, yes, it's me, Freda. I can hear you now. That's better. Hey, how are you?"

"Oh, well, okay, I'm okay, Cammie. Listen, sweetheart, I've been meaning to phone. I wanted to apologize for my behaviour at Marlise's memorial. I was so out of sorts. Just overwhelmed, you know, being there with all of you, and her not there. It was too much for me with everything else. Everything going on."

"Oh, Freda. I'm sorry I haven't been in touch more. I know it's been hard, losing mom, for all of us, but at least we have each other. I didn't realize, or think about, how hard it must be for you still."

Camilla could hear Freda inhaling quick little breaths, stopping back from crying. Trying to stop back.

"I'm sorry, Freda, listen. Would you like to have coffee? I'm free now; kids are gone for the weekend with Noel to visit their gran. Do you mind if I come by?"

"Oh well," Freda said, gasping a little, "I do have someone coming by at three, but yes, that's a ways away still, why don't you come by."

On the way over to Freda's, half an hour into town from Camilla's place, Camilla thought about "the gentleman" Freda had mentioned to Carmen. And about the thing Freda had said about "everything going on." She wondered if it was related to mom somehow, didn't know how she could ask that directly. She thought again about mom telling her she was looking to meet someone that month before she died. And then about mom's dating profile, how she had been hoping to ask Freda about it, wondering about whether it would be appropriate to ask or if it would just upset Freda more. Camilla wondered if mom's profile was still up, if it had been all this time, if these things stayed up even if you weren't active on them. Or if Freda had thought to take it down for mom, seeing as she had been the one to help mom set it up. She would have to find a way to ask Freda. Freda would have known mom talked to her about it. Mom would have said.

Freda answered the door wearing one of her stranger getups. She had always been a bit eccentric. That eccentric aunt. Charmingly so, sort of. She'd always been artsy. Camilla remembers thinking of her as mom's artsy friend, mom's artsy friend sister. They looked so much alike people thought they were sisters. Camilla had sometimes thought of her mom as a toned-down version of her best friend. Maybe the eccentricity had something do with Freda having had more freedom than her mom to express herself, since she'd been more or less a single mom as far back as Camilla could remember, no man to weather remarks from if she seemed to be wearing something out of the ordinary from what was expected of her, the way Camilla had heard her dad do with mom. And even Noel sometimes. Didn't necessarily say anything, but there were looks, or suggestions that she might try something else, something he liked better. Mom would often borrow Freda's jewellery for special events, just an accent to go with something more subtle, not an amalgam of remarkable pieces all mashed together the way Freda wore them. Carmen's dad had never been around much — travelled for work or something for some years, and then just stopped being around. Camilla remembers asking mom about it, but the answer Mom gave was vague, so unlike the very specific way she'd give details about Camilla's dad and his failings. Freda's husband "just stopped coming around," was what mom had said, and "for the better. Freda deserves better." She'd said that too. Freda'd had a couple of steadier boyfriends through the years, and one woman who lived with her for a while after Carmen moved out, maybe a girlfriend, but no one that had ever stayed around long enough to be considered family.

Freda was still artsy, no real surprise, but it had been a while, and Carmen had sort of forgotten so it took her aback. A few weeks ago at the memorial, she had been toned down for Freda. Some kind of grey linen suit. It had hung well on her, looked nice until she had spilled a huge gob of potato salad all over it. Camilla had helped her wash it off while Freda'd cried, "Now look at that! Look what I've gone and done. I've just ruined it. Ruined. It's all just ruined."

Today it was some kind of purple silk elephant suit with green trim. That was the impression Camilla got when Freda opened the door, pendulous folds of purple fabric under her arms like elephant ears, and a green sash draped over her shoulder that looked like a trunk, swaying when Freda opened her arms to hug her. Freda's hair was spiky and silver grey, cut real short up the back and sides, razored even, and pointing straight up like a hedgehog on the top of her head. She had obviously used some kind of glossy pomade to make it shimmer. Not gel, mind you; it wasn't crisp or wet looking, almost looked like it was standing up like that on its own, but Camilla knew enough about hair texture and styling products to suss out Freda's styling regimen. She wore blue eyeliner too. Since the '80s, she had never let up on that. And now it was back in, or had been a few years ago, maybe still was? Camilla wasn't sure. Freda had always worn it. Today it was extra thick, with an emphatic swish at the edges of her eyes that made her look positively catty — still looking relatively sharp despite the smudges of it down her cheeks where she had been rubbing her eyes from crying. My purple aunty elephant cat, Camilla thought, inhaling the familiar patchouli smell of Freda.

"Freda, my dear, you're going to want to clean up a bit, especially if you've got company later," said Camilla, tapping her own cheeks gingerly.

"Oh, oh, am I a mess again? Oh dear, how embarrassing."

"You don't have to be embarrassed, it's just me, Freda; I think if I remember, you wiped my bottom more than enough times that you don't have to be embarrassed in front of me," Camilla replied softly.

"Oh, yes, I did at that. You were sweet then and you're sweet now, Cammie." Freda paused, looking at Camilla lovingly, thin cataract film like opaque glass over her dark brown eyes. "I'll just clean that up, go on in and sit down in the kitchen. I've got coffee on, and some of those snicker-doodles you always liked."

"You're the best, Freda."

Camilla savoured the cinnamon and sugar on her tongue, marvelling at how soft and pillowy Freda's snickerdoodles were, a visceral remembrance of Freda's kitchen.

"Mmhm." Camilla sighed, settling into a restful part of herself she so rarely had time for these days.

"I see you still like them." Freda beamed from the entranceway.

Freda sashayed herself over to the chair opposite Camilla, butterflying her elephant ears to tease a laugh out of Camilla with the particular style of silliness Camilla had always loved about Freda — how she could cut through tension by swaying her body through space, even now such a balance of grace and perfectly executed comedy in the way she performed her aging body. Camilla had always loved watching Freda move.

The two women talked around the weather for a bit, and the road conditions. They talked around Camilla's children and Carmen, Carmen's kids and Camilla's work. Freda seemed normal again, regulated. Like whatever had stricken her was gone. After a short pause in pleasantries, Camilla surprised them both by asking, more directly than she'd meant to, "Freda, I was thinking on the drive over about mom's dating profile. I'd forgotten about it. Her only mentioning it the once to me before she died. Wondering if you'd taken it down, if you'd thought to?"

Freda looked at Camilla in a deeply troubled way, as though Camilla had said something horrific. It was the same troubled look she'd had at mom's memorial, that Camilla had seen for the first time that morning at mom's house—Freda bloodied on the floor, shards of glass glimmering all around her, holding and sobbing over the body of her dear friend. Mom, her dear, dear friend.

And then a knock at the door. Just a few quick raps and the door opening. Cursory raps, someone used to walking in.

"Hello? Marlise? Hello, it's me." A man's voice. An older man. "I'm early, I know, but I woke early and the roads were better than expected . . . oh, I'm sorry, I didn't realize. Oh, I should have. Of course, car on the street out front. Hello."

"Marlise?" Camilla asked, confused.

Freda bolted out of her chair, grabbing the man by the arm, pulling him out of the kitchen, speaking sternly to Camilla, "Stay here, Cammie! I'll be right back."

Camilla started to stand up. "Is everything okay, Fre—" but Freda cut her off before she could finish.

"Everything's fine, Cammie. Stay here, please? I'll be just a moment."

And Freda ushered the man out the door. Had he called her Marlise? Had Camilla misheard that? No, that was what he had said. He had called Freda Marlise, familiarly, intimately, even. What the fuck is going on? thought Camilla, staring out the window at the tree that had grown so much in the years she'd known Freda. The tree she and Carmen used to climb as kids, couldn't even reach the bottom branches now, would need a ladder. There were still remnants of the tree house they had tried building but never really gotten further than a platform. It looked dangerous now. Camilla wondered if Carmen's kids tried to go up there when they visited. She noticed the clothesline wheel too, almost completely encased in bark, clothesline long gone, too much work for Freda to carry the heavy wet basket out and hang the clothes up, she guessed. Maybe Freda had a drying rack like mom had? For silk blouses and undergarments. Things mom never put in the dryer. Camilla threw everything in the dryer. Couldn't be bothered to sort colours, or fabrics. The few things she had that couldn't go in the dryer were so rarely worn that she didn't need a drying rack, just hung them over the shower rod. They had a line, in the summer; she did care about the environment, did her best. But after all those years of washing diapers, after it was over, she just didn't want to deal with a drying rack anymore. She felt a bit guilty every time she pushed the start button on the dryer. Guilty and relieved at the same time. Not having to deal with crispy towels and stinky clothes that didn't dry fast enough, having to wash them again. They had had to throw out the wooden rack they had used then, or burned it? It had gotten mouldy. Probably Noel had burned it. He liked burning things. They hadn't gotten a new one.

Camilla was thinking about the mouldy drying rack when Freda returned.

"I'm sorry, Cammie, I thought Marlo was coming later; I didn't think you'd still be here. I asked him to pick up some things for me at the grocery store, to give us a bit more time because there's something I need to talk to you about. This is hard, Cammie, this is going to be hard. I'm so terribly ashamed of myself, but I can hardly go on pretending anymore. It's gotten out of hand. So out of hand and I don't know how I can fix it now, or change it. I do need some help. Maybe you are the one to help me after all, though I do feel so terribly guilty."

"Did he call you Marlise, Freda? Did I hear him call you Marlise?"

"Yes, yes, he did call me Marlise. He thinks I am Marlise. That's what I mean, Cammie. He doesn't know your mom is dead; he thinks I'm her. This is going to be hard for me, so please, let me go through it; can you listen, just listen while I try to make my way through it all, no questions?"

"I'll do my best, Freda, though I do have an awful lot of questions right now."

"I understand, Cammie, just let me finish, and then you can ask whatever you want and I'll try to answer. I've asked Marlo to give me another hour, so we have a bit of time before he comes back. And if you're still here, I don't want you to tell him. I do want to tell him, but I need to figure out how. Maybe you can help me do that, figure out how to tell him, once you hear the story."

"This sounds messed up, Freda."

"Very messed up, Cammie. It's been messed up since Marlise died. And I just seem to keep messing it up more.

"It all started with your mom's dating profile. The one you were asking about, that I'd help her put up on Silver Singles. To answer your question, yes, I have taken it down. But I didn't. Not right away after she died. I meant to, but instead something else happened. We were celebrating that night. The night she died. She had been exchanging messages with Marlo for weeks. 'Marlo and Marlise, imagine that,' she'd said to me, 'like two peas in a pod.' Things got romantic fast. You know, when you're older, maybe you think you might not have as much time, or at least that's what your mom had said, that she'd wasted so much time already. He wrote such beautiful things to her, and he was handsome, as you saw. She shared them all with me, of course. I wanted to make sure she was being careful. We were like schoolgirls, her and I, like we were in it together, really. Me, I had gone through that so many times through the years, you know, that first burgeoning of love, the excitement of getting to know someone new, but your mom, well she'd been with your dad so long. She'd forgotten. It was like a dream coming true for her. Marlo, dear, sweet Marlo. He gave her a lot of happiness before she died, you know. She fell in love with him after only a few weeks of messages, and then they were gifted a few months more. She was deeply in love, the way you can feel about someone when they haven't had the time to do or say anything yet that makes you doubt them. They had made plans to meet in person. We had planned it together, were going to meet up with him together while we were in Victoria for the trip she and I had planned to see the Royal Winnipeg Ballet's *Dracula*. Oh, you remember, you had bought her ticket for her, hadn't you?"

Camilla listened to Freda telling this story. A story about her mom, and it fascinated her to hear Freda talk this way. So openly, like she had heard her mom and Freda talk all their lives. But it seemed absurd too, made up somehow, like the whole time since her mom had mentioned her dating profile had all been a dream, was still a dream, and maybe her mom still was alive and she'd just been dreaming this all along. These thoughts arose for Camilla, arose and receded as she listened to Freda's story about a part of mom's life that had never happened to mom, but instead had happened to Freda. Happened by accident to Freda, because mom had died.

"We agreed I'd go with her to meet Marlo, to make sure it was safe. The two of us. So he was expecting two of us. You can never be too safe with strangers on the internet, know for sure they are who they say they are. Well, haven't I proven that! But Marlo was who he said he was, or I'm pretty certain by now he is who he says he is. Although he's probably certain I am who I say I am too. But I'm not, am I?"

And then Freda had stopped, staring out the window, something catching her eye. It was the sun, the sun shining off that old clothesline pulley, almost completely absorbed into the tree by now.

Home (in Four Parts)

Sorrow

I am very certain of my sorrow. My sorrow has a hard back. Its bones have been compacted to an unyielding block, clamped from all my holding. My sorrow is made from bone and biopolymer that I think of as pressed birch-bark, holding the length of me together so I might float instead of drown. Instead of being sleek though, I am shaped like an aging monkey. A sad old lab monkey who has spent her life as the subject of experiments devised by crafty scientists who do not believe in any God. How could they? Cutting into the monkey's flesh with small scalpels and inserting nodes into her to test the curiosities of brain chemistry and electromagnetic impulses through nerve fibres? Drawing extrapolations from her somewhat similar design to speculate on our own patterned impulses of sadness, elation, and shot fire rage.

None of it having anything to do with God, this substitution and conjecture—Her sense of humour and brutal honesty that have gotten so out of hand now that she is a little bit crazy with all this new heat. It gets too much for Her, so she rips off all Her clothes to breathe for just a few eons, panting and unable to care about anything other than relief from these flushes. While power-hungry men chew all the rich meat then toss us the bones, thinking we should be grateful, distracted by our fatty mouths while the world dies off and they keep drafting up contracts to raze all that is green to make way for progress. Then sell green back to us just a little bit brighter and a lot less living than it was before.

She's just so hot she can't think straight. What did She put all this stuff here for anyway? And those lessons to live a good life by? The stories? How they got snuffed out of the children's mouths with myths and brutalities designed to acclimatize us to Truth according to another people's stories.

How our stories survived in an innate knowledge of ice. To be retold—now with lisps and blips and sorrow in them. Now with force. Now with love. For those in whom memory arises, for those called toward listening to songs heard through time.

Happiness

Looking back on the wending of my sorrow, I imagine an epitaph:

Think of the trauma you inflicted on the world by virtue of your standing-ovation happiness.

Then pencil for my former self, and other selves like me a tale:

How you were always in need of a squad to assure you, how your happiness surpassed all other needs. How you were deserving of this happiness. Bloody well deserving of a good life and all its trappings. So you bought a bigger house with big windows and installed state-of-the-art surveillance equipment, a home gym, an entertainment suite, had a well-recommended children's room designer consult with the kids to co-design their personal living spaces, replete with educational, entertainment, and creative success-oriented gender motifs. To model a good life.

Make the model and the life will follow. Sprinkle it with the new neon dust from the cake-decorating shop on the corner where the community radio used to be. Make it too beautiful to eat. Take a picture of it and cross-post it to as many sites as possible, so users can pin, share, link, repost, attesting to your epic taste! Emoticon the shit out of it, so everyone knows you also feel things.

Once in a dream you asked your analyst what the difference would be if you lived a life without models driving you? Instead crafted something else? It was a weird question and the analyst looked like a bird with deep black eyes and a chasm mouth when you asked it. You think the answer was a deep long caw that flattened everything in its path but forgot it when you awoke to the ding of your smart phone announcing this morning's recipe for maple-and-marmalade-glazed French toast with whipped coconut cream and salted strawberries. And satisfaction flooded you as you thought of the girls delicately forking the succulent stacks into their pretty mouths. You texted them the pic and told them to meet you downstairs, *asap*! And your mind snapped back to your happiness project, reminding you that you *can* bully life by lining up all the chattel and transforming it into a mirage to homestead your sophisticated wants over the fabric of the everyday. Make it real by envisioning. Visions mass-produced in magazines, television shows, popular blogs, and self-help books assuring you of your right to *this* wealth, and the walls needed to uphold it. Yum!

Camaraderie

Rust is so tricky to name. It's always flaking away on you. Bit of water bit of air, and bam! You get what you're going for, sort of. That weathered look, the old-timey feel. Then you have to shellac the fence so it doesn't flake off onto the walkway and drag into the house on your shoes. Or poison some shit-ass toddler who licks it when his mom is busy updating her status with a photo of him, doe-eyed near a freshly popped crocus a few minutes before. And you're liable for that because it's on your property, holding the sidewalk back from your garden, making sure passersby understand that they can look but not cross over.

You've got little signs low down aimed at the dog walkers who are tempted to let their friends piss on your luscious peonies. Real polite signs that say *Please!* So the neighbours won't feel alienated by you asking them to take their dog to piss elsewhere while they consider how you've come to capture rust and allow it to reflect so much light, how it is that everything within your borders flourishes, how they're invited to look but not touch. Look but not leave deposits behind.

How a little bit it's the rust that holds you all together but you don't understand how until your mother visits and tells you a story about iron oxide, earth, and the making of pigments. She tells you her grandmaman told her when she was a little girl before she left home, then spins into some strange discussion about blood and the bodies of women and all the stains left behind on all the beds you ever slept in during the bleeding years of your life. The sweet bold smell, the dizziness. Crusted-up scars on the knees of children allowed to pedal their bikes as fast as they can down all the dirt roads of the world.

Your mother wants to know why you are trying to capture and stall rust, about the kind of shellac you used, and how often you'll have to touch up. She wants to know if you are still bleeding, or if you're past that now and maybe this is why the rusted railing? She asks how it is that you have no shame in your lack of love for the neighbours, and wonders if it is because you were born during those years when women were encouraged not to breastfeed and not hold their babies too much, lest the babies become attached in aberrant ways and stretch their mothers' boobs out. She thinks it might be because she drank too much, though she's sober now, and her boobs still look spectacular. She encourages you to eat more meat. She encourages you to listen to jazz. She tells you her sex life has flourished now that your father is dead and there are so many singles at the Gracious Living home who have nothing to lose with their bodies. She tells you that after all these years, she is paying homage to the bodies of women, coaxing curiosity from the otherwise latent members of some of the men in her choir, men who for years had been struggling with dysfunction. She tells you she has been reading articles online about pleasure and attempts to guide you through some pelvic exercises intended to increase your orgasmic potential. She tells you it is your birthright. All through this you are squeezing so hard with every muscle of your body, trying to shut her out without appearing disrespectful, because she is emotionally sensitive and you do not want to clamp down on her freedoms with your sorrow, although you wonder if her hard-won freedoms have something to do with where your sorrow came from in the first place. Instead of pleasure, you are left afterward with a strained jaw, cramped fingers, and stuck toes while your mother smiles blissfully. *Rust*, you whisper to yourself as you clamp, *rust, rust, rust.*

Padding through the halls in soft pumps

I tell my mother, "Suffice it to say we are broken."

"Ha!" she says, "when have we ever not been broken?"

I try to trace all the stories I've been given back through time and find layers and layers of discomfort. Layers and layers of trying to gloss over why we are here and how we are here and the methods of our relations. Sealant meant to keep some things crystal clear, holes in the backyard where the compost was left to rot back into earth. A whole lot of static.

Those ancestors who were already here, who had spent so much time becoming themselves with the land. Those ancestors who arrived here not knowing, wanting to learn only what they could make theirs. Make a story about how those who were already here weren't really here because they did not parcel and chop up the land, laying claim through appropriation. Making home out of that. Then legislating unlearning in order to alienate the land. All the messy God stuff fucked into the bodies of men in black robes. The mixing up of the ancestors and stuffing cotton wads in the mouths of some of them to keep them quiet about who they are. Scaring the shit out of everyone with guilt and shame and hell. So much brutality and suffering. So much piety and propriety. All the clacking of teeth, all the nightmares whispered through the confessional to men with greedy bones haunted by all sorts of demons gilded over with verse.

These vague impressions of family.

She tells me to stop asking so many questions. We are where we are now and these are not my stories, she says. "Those are my stories, not yours. *Ils ne t'appartiennent pas.*"

She left to get away from them, raise her children free from Church and the ravages of family. Family ravaged by Church.

The stories circle like a pack of snappy coyotes and I do not know why they are always nipping around at our heels as my sisters and I go about our lives trying to live up to her maxim: Think only good things so only good things come.

"Pensez seulement aux bonnes choses et seulement les bonnes choses vont arriver."

She knows it's a lie but repeats it nonetheless. Reminds me when I try to talk about how I cannot breathe sometimes and my sister's veins have popped all over her arms, hard to find a good place these days for the needles. My mother paints a mural on her wall using various hues of ochre. She tells me the shiny parts are where the spirit is always seeping into us if we are only able to look.

She insists that I am to hear but not repeat— "Not yours to tell." Listen, very quietly.

It took her a very long time to be able to speak without fear of being annihilated, so it's important that I know the truth, she tells me, but do not go about trying to tell it. She used all her powers to keep our bodies safe from predatory men for as long as she wielded power over how we used our bodies in the world. She wants us to understand her better, even though we never can. Know where she came from but don't ever, not ever think of going there ourselves. Forget any inklings of reconnection. Forget the idea that we might belong somewhere where the ancestors remember us.

"How do we slough off stories told too many times, unearth ones that haunt our family behind stuffed mouths?" I ask her.

"Not secrets," she says, though some of her family deny them. "Just not your stories."

She wants to sing new songs (those tunes though, they do stick), doesn't want to keep coughing through the trauma, as though those are the only stories. She squeezes and squeezes and her hardened face transforms into blissful distance. The smoke helps.

Is it enough to change the words? Is it enough to stuff them in a sack and drown them like unwanted kittens? What about the ghosts that come back as kitten men to haunt our dreams and fill our children's play with disturbing likenesses to our deeply buried fears? Is it true, for instance, that there was a time before this one, when things were better than they are? Could we separate ourselves from these entanglements, blended into lumpy mush as we are?

Take for instance my first-grade teacher, Mrs. Kleiber. I knew nothing about her and still know nothing about her, not even her first name. I liked Mrs. Kleiber because she was pretty enough, but not disturbingly so. In my mind this had something to do with her being nice. She wore shoes that clacked down the hall, soft sensible pumps that gave her purchase on the linoleum tiles for a fast walk but slowed her down so she could not break into a run without slipping. We saw that the time Buck Mussel pushed Dee Smith and she smashed her tooth through her lip. Mrs. Kleiber picked her up and tried to run with her to the office where they kept the first-aid things, but she slipped and the blood smeared all over the beige floor when Dee fell again.

We all stood around looking at it until Mr. Harlow came and rounded us up, back into the classroom.

The red stain mixed up things for me that were meant to be kept separate. Dee Smith's blood on the outside of her body. Dee Smith's blood on the almost-white floor. Buck Mussel didn't come back to our class after that. They put him in the special class with the other special kids and the special teacher. The special kids had a different recess so we didn't see him out there when there were no adults around. Dee Smith got black stitches and her lip swelled up. Later she had a white scar on her brown skin that I wanted to touch but knew I shouldn't. A few years later, when I was sure it had healed, I traded her a mandarin orange for a gentle stroke, running my index finger down from her bottom lip to the divot below. It was bumpy and thick feeling and made my knees feel squidgey. My world washed out with a red stain, and I saw then what I had not seen the first time — a red-breasted bird flying up from the smear of blood, down the corridor, and out the window — somehow understanding that something of Dee had loosed itself to the world and although her body had been sealed up, there was part of her out there nesting in trees and pulling up fat worms, doing bird things while Dee was inside learning her times tables. Maybe it had been there all along and Dee just wasn't telling.

When I was almost old enough to understand that the world becomes more confusing the longer I live in it, I learned that Dee Smith had another name that she went home to. And another language at home different from my home language and different from the one all around us in the mouths of the teachers and children, other stories that did not fit at all with the stories she was learning about her home at school.

Dee Smith understood early that there are different kinds of truths. Her blood turned into a bird and flew outside. I wanted to eat ice cream and Dee wanted to eat ice cream. I buried insects and made little graves for them and Dee learned the names of her relations spread out over the land. I learned to shoot a gun and hit my dad's beer cans and Dee learned how to clean and cut and hang the fish for smoking. How to make the fire. I wore a *My Little Pony* T-shirt and Dee wore a *My Little Pony* T-shirt and I thought we were the same but Dee knew we were not. Even though I knew I wasn't the same as Buck Mussel or Krista Sloan, or any of the other girls with nice ponytails and brand new clothes, I thought I might be a little bit the same as Dee Smith. When she let me see the bird in her that one time I understood that she knew who she was in a way I did not, and I became a little bit afraid of her. I wanted a bird in me and when I got one, a ruffed grouse that danced and stomped, my mother put a stop to its powers by telling me it was only pretend. By showing me the identification guides that gave it a Latin name and certain instinctual behaviours. Behaviours it could not otherwise itself out of now that it had been taxonomically named and categorized. Habits and habitats, firm solid boundaries that cannot be crossed over. The grouse could not become me. I could not follow her into the forest to scratch up seeds. My mother forbade it.

"Some things," she said, "are not yours to know."

The bird and I were separate worlds, worlds my mother sat on the borders of to make sure I could not pass. She wanted me to know that it existed, and I was meant to have respect for, but not become curious about its world.

When Dee was a child she knew she was not separate worlds from her bird, even though Mrs. Kleiber would have told her she was. Everything she had to learn she had to learn through teeth. Air sucking through to let learnings of different orders pass over and not internalize them as shame as they clashed about trying to define who she was. Dee's family taught her how to be proud so even though she heard a lot of noise out there in the big-people world, setting her teeth to grinding or rattling, she knew how to suck and taste with her tongue on her insides to remind herself of her birdness, to remind herself the shame was not hers to carry. It was one of her powers to shift imperceptibly when there was danger nearby. To know how dangerous certain kinds of kindness could be.

I moved away from Dee Smith's home and now I am here with this garden. Now I am here with this rust. Now I am here with this life full of pockmarks and pubic hair that my cleaner does away with so I can go on living at the surface of things, with all the surface of things designed to resemble beauty. It is never enough to fill me up, but I am good at pretending I know how to be where I am on this land I own that does not belong to me. With the stories I've been given that I'm not allowed to tell.

Part Two

Housekeeping

The Leopard in the Bathroom

My mother encounters a leopard in the bathroom and beats it to within an inch of its life. My father, walking in the door after night shift, curses at her for not finishing the job. Now there's this half-dead leopard in the bathroom, and who is going to have to deal with that? Already twelve hours spent hauling coal, and now this heaping mass of dangerous flesh ready to tear his being to shreds.

He decides to ignore it. Throws the baby blue bath mat with black dog fur felted all into the weave over the beast's face. The blood pools upward. He watches the spot spread as he takes his morning shit. Chest rising and falling, rising and falling, gasping for breath.

Just a bloodstained bath mat on the bathroom floor, not his job to take care of that. Months he could go, years, stepping out of the shower onto the mat without feeling he should do anything about it. He washes his hands and looks at his face, coal dust lining the creases of his eyes, stuck under his fingernails, little flecks of it staining the sheets grey where his body imprints when he sleeps.

For a week my sisters and I go out back behind the trailer to pee on account of that dying leopard. We hold ourselves, until the bus drops us off at school, to take a crap without fear of getting a leg bit off.

Then one day the leopard is gone and mom and dad are talking to each other again like it had never been there. The mat's been washed but there's still this faint rust-grey stain, shaped like a spent peony, drooping from the spot where the leopard's keen eye had been.

Reflections for Rita-Mae
on Her Fortieth Birthday

A little sticky note on the front cover of the booklet, scrawled in Chrissy's handwriting reads:

> Hey girl! It's a doozy, we spent some time on this for you, wanting to celebrate the bigness of it. Louise made the book and we all got together for a craft night without inviting you (sorry!) so we could each art up our pages. Lola laid it out with our "vignettes" and got it printed. Hope you feel the love!

Vignette 1
Lola: As much happiness as is given over to ravens
(Collage of two ravens cut from Peterson's 1947 *A Field Guide to the Birds* atop black and white photograph of Rita-Mae's high school graduation photo. Background:

cut strips of cloth from Rita-Mae's discarded wedding
dress hand-stitched into the paper and embroidered
with forget-me-nots, some of it tea-dyed to look
like earth, worked through with bits of wool—worms
digging through eyelets.)

As much happiness as is given over to ravens. As much grief. As much playfulness as they lob their bodies through invisible currents of sky. As much hope as is given to eagles, to hunt the rivers day after day. As much sorrow to cows, whose calves are shot in the fields beside them, who continue to give us milk, the same fingers that pull down on their teats, pressed decidedly on the trigger, jarred from the kickback. As much dirt as is pushed through a worm's gut, coming out as casing through the hole on the other end. And the beautiful aeration of earth in that, the delicious gift for all the roots searching below ground. The beetles who travel the wormways, grateful for a bit of movement without having to do all the pushing themselves.

As much tenderness as is given to surgeons, when they cut through delicate skin, precisely through thick muscle, making the opening just big enough to pull out the babies. As much consternation as is given to babies who suck in air for the first time, the cool harshness of it in place of amniotic fluid the same temperature as the fetus's own lungs. As much and not more as the slip of the egg from the chicken's cloaca, the perfect blueness left behind in the nesting box.

As much static as passes for the presence of other humans when the radio shifts out of range the farther you drive away from any small northern town. The static between places, the static of space.

The set of the jaw that comes with age, the hardnesses of life, smiles forced through something that sticks, unlike the easy joy that beams through the unencumbered face of the child. The same child also sulking in unencumbered grief. Different words for anger. Different words for joy. Different words for sadness. All of them important in understanding the range of a life. Develop happiness by learning the different words for anger. Find humour in the slightness between rage and fury, displeasure and disgust. The itchy place between irascibility and ire. The lofty lunge between vexation and wrath. Pop! Just a bit of bubbling sound through the otherwise clenched gut, sounds like a guffaw rolling over to giggle, gasped back into a sob, tumbled through an emergent softness into a frolicking titter. The affective dance of rooted entities in the emotive forces of relation. Hormonal highways rocking us as we breathe, sneeze, touch, taste, hear, see, sense the pulsing world.

Vignette 2
Chrissy: Squeal and fist pump
(Matte photographs printed from internet, hand-cut, collaged, digitally scanned, and reprinted: two women standing in the front seat of a 1964 Oldsmobile

Starfire convertible with the top down, lifting legs
up in frilly dresses to expose vintage bloomers,
desert landscape open and calling from beyond.)

Rolling down a hill then rolling up a hill. You have to go
over it if you want to get to the top and see what's on the
other side. Isn't the downward side the cruising part? Like
the first part is all struggle and you work your ass off and
shit and then you just sit back and enjoy the scenery? Why
the sense that once you're over the good part's done? Kick
your feet up, Rita-Mae, honey, the tough part's over, no
more bullshit now you get to unapologetically squeal and
fist pump all the way to the other side!

Vignette 3
Hilary: Bright linen tunics
(Watercolour painting of magenta tunic with orange
swirl on white background.)

You slide into your fifth decade and look down at your body,
thinking *What the fuck?* Or *Goddamn, girl!* Or maybe something more like *Oh?* Or *Bhgleghck-hhhaurgh...?* Yup, it's your
body all right, not the same as it's always been. More wrinkles, to be sure, and you know they're just getting started.
They're going to spread now, just like your hips, and your
boobs and your skin. Everything is going to loosen up.
That's the fun part. Loosening up. You don't have to worry

anymore about whether you're going to shack up and find a mate and make some beautiful babies. You don't have to worry if your ass looks good in those jeans, not really. I mean, you might still worry, but you shouldn't, because let's be honest, even if people are looking, they're not looking in the same way they used to. And you don't want them to either, even if you might want the memory of the elation and uncertainty it used to give you, like your ass in the jeans might tip over the scales of a life, one way or another. Now you just hope there isn't dried crud on your jeans, or if there is, that it's not too visible, that your soft little tum isn't drooping over the waistline in a way that digs in so you have to shift uncomfortably in your seat. It's not like when you were wearing them so tight you couldn't breathe and had to sit upright to make sure there was no internal damage; they just might be ill-fitting because you don't even know anymore what size you're supposed to wear after all the swelling and shrinking of the last few years. You can relax now, maybe even wear linen? Seems like something to do once you hit forty, make a change to loose linen after all the years of stretch cotton and denim. I've even ordered you a loose flowing tunic that will come soon in the mail. Please text me a photo of you wearing it once you get it. I got it from a boutique for distinguished women; bright colours are in this year and I know you'll look fabulous in magenta-orange swirl!

Vignette 4

Bobbi: A robot story

(Split page—on one side, a line drawing of robot woman looking pleased but innocent; on the other side, a sad-looking deconstructed paper doll with toddler snot on her.)

You know I'm not there yet, and to be honest, I'm kind of dreading it. But this is for you and not about me and I want to give you something to look forward to, or at least something that's not all about feelings of loss pushed at you hard from a culture obsessed with youth. You know, even the aging beauties we see photos of all plasticized, or at least airbrushed so the wrinkles and sags get smoothed out. Leaving maybe just a few tasteful-looking lines that make a face look happy. And you know me well enough to know I'll do anything to stay as fresh as I can for as long as I can, fighting age with as much bravado as I put into my spin classes. Pushing as hard as I can for as long as I can until my legs turn to jelly and I can barely walk from the pulsing heat of my muscles thumping hard with my oxygen-enlivened blood.

So I'll give you a little story about a robot named Marisa, or Maurice, who has always wanted to feel human. This robot is a bit slower to learn than a flesh human of equivalent age. She has to try things over and over again because even though her computer brain is a lot better at storing information and putting thoughts together, her somatosensory system is sluggish. We're just not really there yet in terms of robots. She isn't as graceful as her human companion Pelinda, who by forty has developed a real grace in her movements, mastering things like ravioli making and typing. Marisa/Maurice is just getting started on life at forty. Up to now it was all just infancy. And Pelinda, she's working on another coming of age too, preparing for the next bump. Last few years of normal menstruation before the hormonal flux of menopause racks the body with all sorts of curiosities of selfhood. Get ready, girl, it's coming, adolescence in reverse! Some years of an erratic endocrine before the calmness of the crone years set in.

Let's be honest though, Marisa/Maurice is not really forty, she's just programmed to think she is. Because she's a robot she can live in time differently than humans, processing experiences that much faster. So she's got forty years of living under her belt, but not forty years of wear and tear on her body. Machines wear down faster than biological beings who've got some sort of neat regeneration shit going on in their cellular structures. We haven't figured that out yet with self-healing technology, so she'd probably be all gummed up at forty, leaking fluids all over the place, having to participate in antique shows, and needing a special licence plate, only drive on weekends and not in the dark, that kind of thing. Maybe the way it works is that they keep moving her subjectivity from one model to the next when the first one wears out? Each time she has to learn a new body, but the models keep getting more precise, so it's like upgrading each time? She gets to retain the expertise of the first model and apply it to the next. Now that's progress!

Maurice/Marisa remembers and learns and does things, always with increasing prowess, but her emotions are wacky, clownish even. It's like she's always over- or under-doing things because she has to make a choice about her emotions, pick which one to send coursing through her body, clenching her up or opening her face into a look of beaming joy. For Pelinda it's the other way around. The thought process and the naming of feeling come after the body's expression. Marisa/Maurice is a bit off, but she's a robot, and well-intentioned, so people forgive her for it.

I guess I don't really know where I was going with that robot thing. I wanted to give you a bit of hope, something simple to wish you well, make the next bit of life seem exciting, like the way things were when you were eighteen and away from home for the first time and waking up every morning felt like your whole life was before you, every person you met a possible life-changer, every new street in a new city some kind of metaphor grabbing at your soul, as yet uncharted. The fledgling maps in your independent psyche throbbing with romantic beauty, and you at the centre of it all. But thing is, when you get to where you are you've been kicked and punched all over with loss and long-ing, so that kind of raw confusing magic has petered out, or

at least been channelled so it's not flooding all over everything, maybe just tinging things here and there, slapping
you in the face once in a while when you're not expecting
it. The kids, so much of your magic has gone into them that
you always ache a bit when they're not there, even though
you long for yourself without them, strategizing with inces-
sant effort to parcel time out just for you. I wanted the robot
to show that it isn't a loss, this channelling of magic. Use
her to demonstrate Pelinda's emotional sophistication, the
way the oscillations of enchantment have spread out, so
she's not hung up in them, getting flung about like a paper
doll drenched in toddler snot and dropped out a fourth-
story window. Not flat but undulating, the way as you've
gotten older you listen to instrumental jazz rather than
warehouse riot grrrl punk hammered all over with static
and indignation.

Vignette 5
Louise: Technological dreaming
(Bright Technicolor gouache palette rectangle strip
set atop faded-out colour palette rectangle strip.)

Everything I have dreamed in the last ten years has been
dreamed in colour. The people, I mean, coloured into muted
landscapes, also in colour, but washed out. Like old photographs in which the people have been coloured in, but the
colours of the people in my dream aren't overhued greens

and reds like in the photographs, they're high definition, sharper than what my eyes can actually see, as though I'm looking at actors on a computer screen. The actors in my dreams look like the people I know, but better. Cheekbones a little sharper, creases less deep, skin less ruddy, pounds of flesh skimmed off. So when I wake, the people around me are always slightly disappointing. Too used looking, all roughed up by life. I look at them and can't help but want my dream people back.

So I just want you to know that about dreaming after forty. That the possibilities for brightness are there, you just have to find sleep to get them. I'm not sure what it means about the roughed-up used-looking real-lifers, because shit, those are the ones we have to love, aren't they? But no one says you can't have an active dream world while you're doing all the work of keeping a life together! And when I'm lucky, after a real hard day, my real-lifers will show up in my dreams and I get to forgive them for being imperfect, and then love them better the next day. It's true I never really see myself in the dream world, so I don't get that extra colour and sharpness, but who can really see themselves anyway?

A Home for Secrets

She gets a secret goat. She hides it in the barn. She has to do it secretly. But the secret goat needs fresh air and fodder and needs to be attended to. And the secret goat needs company so she has to get a second secret goat, and a secret pair of pigeons. She has to make a good pen for them, and good sleeping quarters because wolves and martens are so good at figuring out secrets. They'll sniff right through her veneers and grab her secret goats by the throats, tear off her pigeons' heads while they're roosting. So she's got to do some secret building to make sure everyone is safe. And only then, once it's all good and done, once there's no way to come along and say it isn't possible, once all the items on the list he'll bring up about all the things he doesn't want to have to deal with have been checked off, because she's done them all herself without his help, only then can she live her secret life of goat-tending.

The children are unhelpful in her secret life. They ask for things constantly; they watch everything she does and want to be a part of it. They'll talk about the goat and the preparations if they're made privy to them. Keeping secrets from the children is harder than keeping secrets from him. So she invents a secret door that needs a secret key. And then because children are very interested in secret doors and secret keys, she has to invent things that are repulsive to them. Repulsive but not repulsively titillating, otherwise they will put all their efforts into getting close to the secret. So the secret door and secret key get a trick to them.

The children are small enough that they do not understand clockwise and counter-clockwise. They do not understand clicks and turns and tricks. So the key has to go counter-clockwise and click through three notches to open the real secret door. The pretend secret door opens after just one clockwise click, and this she shows them. It goes to a room in the barn that is just a pretend secret, where she has put all sorts of things that the children are fascinated with. She has to change these things constantly or the children will lose interest. It takes a lot of time, time she needs for the building of the goats' secret home, but if she doesn't do this, the children will make it impossible for her to have her secrets.

She tells the children she must go out of the pretend secret room to do boring things that are repulsive to them, but she has to be very careful in the things she chooses, because the things adults find repulsive are often of interest to small children. Because children want to try everything, they just do not want to try it for very long. She tells them she is going to make meals they do not want to eat, or tidy up messes they have made. She makes the pretend secret room more interesting than the things she is doing, and in this way the things she is doing become repulsive. She can hear the children in their pretend secret room while she is in her real secret room. She puts a doll of herself in there because they are very interested in her and the things they can do on her body. This doll they are able to jump on, and flop around, and feed or pile dirt on. The doll is soft and snuggly so they can snuggle her and call her mama. They think it is very funny to have a doll mama and a real mama. In the house they are not allowed to play with doll mama, they can only play with her in the pretend secret room, a prohibition that makes doll mama who lives in the barn feel very, very special. Real mama sets up novel scenarios for doll mama that the children discover every time they open the secret door. So much time is spent with this charade that she moves forward very slowly in her preparations.

She has made the secret preparations and hidden the goats and pigeons. Now she must find a way to build them secretly into their lives without his knowing so that he cannot say they are making life more difficult. Once they have been incorporated into their life without making it more stressful than it already is then they can stop being secret and all the curiosity, joy, milk, fertility, death, meat, and friendship they bring can be revealed to him without his thinking it will only be a burden. The adaptation will not be one of responsibilities that he does not want more of, just of revelation that all this time she has been living a secret life of goat-tending while also being all the other things she is in the home they share with their children.

Understanding Groceries

A thought Brenda scrawls in the grocery notebook:

The bell rings happily; it's more than we ever wanted.
More than we ever wanted. When all we wanted was
this blue light. Blue light to last forever, an ongoing,
unending hopefulness. Living in the liminality of that
without ever losing pace. Forgiveness rolling from us
like rain off waxy poplar leaves, beading to trickles.
Instead of this constant mass of frustrations, sharply
expelled hisses in the realm of our loves.

Patterns explode, indicating presence. Before the blue
light became this almost whiteness; anything was
possible. It was like not knowing, but not knowing
with the grittiest glee of possibility arising out of every
keen pore. Skin tilted to that which might come.

Day arrives and we are beholden to its sentiments. The
dishes, the dishes, the dishes. The wet soapy water
for washing our grime. Ongoing heroics of grime
annihilation—though she always gets the better of us
in the end. We wear our hands rough with the bravery
of resistance. Until we die and she converts us back
into herself by the action of the creepy-crawlies she
sends forth in endlessness. Life to food to waste, to
life to food to waste to life, all of it teeming and filthy.
Trick of light to whisk our days to cleanliness, making
us furious or dutifully aligned to service, depending
how the light falls.

A peek into Brenda's life:

Brenda wakes up happy, thinking the clock reads six. She is
happy for seven minutes working through the dream that
is sticking to her consciousness, trying to make sense of the
dance that opened a portal to elsewhere, a way to always
get away from where she was as long as she could find the
place to step into and dance the dance properly. She never
knew in the dream whether she was really dancing properly. Either she was going to be lucky enough or she wasn't.

It turned out she was, but only after a lot of worrying.
Only after the last minute when the ones that were coming
to get her were almost there and the flight she had to catch

was about to leave without her. It seemed like she was going to make it. Someone called to tell her where to look. Someone was looking out for her, though it was up to her to make the right moves, otherwise it would all fall apart and she would be trapped by enemies into something terrible. She never dreamed what the terrible was, just that it was impending. Always this impending terribleness. Which was terrible in itself. Terrible enough, thought Brenda. But she was still happy to have been dancing in her dream, to have had someone helping her this time, to have a way out.

After seven minutes Brenda glances at the clock: 5:07! Barely after five. Brenda does not want to be awake at barely after five, but her toddler is already sucking back his milk. There's no getting him back to bed now.

And just like that, Brenda loses hope.

Her happiness changes to desperation. She trudges to the kitchen to heat water for tea, to give her a small immediate hit of strength to attend to the toddler's morning rituals before she can pause long enough to clean out the coffee machine, grind the beans, and gently heat the cream for her morning coffee without being assailed with books needing to be read "right now!," more milk, a snack, and having to be present in the bathroom while he poops because he's scared of the monsters in there.

She would have gone to bed earlier and not been sleep deprived if her husband had not cornered her before bed to talk about finances.

He is always worried about finances. He tries to figure out a formula that will make finances become a comprehensible thing that no longer causes him worry. As though laying the numbers out a certain way will make it clear how to know for sure where to spend money and where not to. As though you could cost out the future and know that it will all be okay because it was built into the budget. It always is okay and never seems that it will be. That's the way it was with her father growing up, and that's the way it is with her husband now. Finances make her want to hide in her little shell and do turtle things until all the talking is over.

Brenda hides money all over the house in places he will never look as a buffer against his anxieties. She does not know what kind of buffers he has against her anxieties but thinks his special ability to pretend he is listening when he really is not—because he doesn't seem to remember so many of the things she tells him—is one of the ways he tries to maintain himself amidst her daily struggles. She knows his budgets are like her dream dancing, some kind of portal to an okay elsewhere in which terribleness is not always impending. She figures out her own secret calculations and goes on doing things the way she wants to do them while he roils about in financial insecurity. He doesn't want to work more or for more money, and it wouldn't matter if he did; the numbers would always come out the same way, even if they increased dramatically. The cost of things would just go up, always balancing out to the same place. Or at least that's what people tell her who have a lot more money than they do and always worry about not having enough. And she knows it's a little bit true from her own fluctuating money worlds. Sometimes she has enough to buy cheese and sometimes she doesn't. Cheese tastes good either way, and if they don't have any to eat, there are other things she can make and it gives her something to look forward to, like maybe next time she goes shopping there'll be enough for cheese, and then she can eat a grilled cheese for lunch!

Brenda thinks maybe he would feel better with a cushion there? She gets a little bit hopeful thinking she could make life better for him, and in that way make life better for her family, if she could put her cheese money into a super-secret place for him? Sew a pouch into one of the couch cushions and put a five, ten, or twenty in there, depending on what kind of cheese she was thinking of buying and didn't? And they could watch his cushion slowly grow?

Only Brenda knows cushions can catch on fire or get covered in baby vomit and you can never get the smell out of them so you have to throw them out or live with the milky pungency every time you try to rest your head down. So she hedges her bets with piles of toonies in shoeboxes for shoes that no longer fit her swollen feet, and folded-up fives in a Mason jar behind the face cloths on the top shelf of the linen closet. She decides to stick with buying the cheese when she can. And still ends up once a month with a spare twenty she keeps flattened between the pages of her feminist-theory books. She must have close to a grand stuffed in the collected works of Haraway, hooks, and Irigaray by now. She knows he'll never look there.

There are other little caches too. Sometimes he finds them and she acts surprised, thanking him for finding her misplaced Christmas money. Sometimes she spends the money on things for the children that have not been included in the budget, or more books that she tries to sneak into the house without him seeing so that he will not complain about having too many books in the house or too many toys or collectibles that achieve nothing but dust collection and inspirations of whimsy.

She inherited the secret caching from her mother, who filled their childhood with wonder from little scrounged chunks that were nestled away from the calculating limits of budget—her mother stretching a teeny bit what was actually possible. When there was so much that was out of reach, unaffordable, not for us. Every once in a while her mother would find a way to pop these small things out of the beyond. Then Brenda and her sisters would rejoice, hopping around like crazed things for the sweet luck of life. They would bounce with gratitude until the gratitude wore off and they would start to fight over the things that each coveted from the other.

A thought Brenda scrawls in the grocery notebook:

Living together as a nuclear family in a walled-in house is like constantly burning little fires that aren't put out properly and stepping on the hot ashes in the most surprising of moments. Moments in which you were almost certain the air around you was free of smoke and all the fires had been put out and the ashes swept into the garden compost to feed next year's plants. Then all over your feet are these pustulant blisters. They stink a little and weep constantly. The fancy creams rubbed erotically onto freshly shaved shiny legs on television do nothing but sting when you try to lovingly stroke yourself back into prettiness.

You do not understand motherly prettiness. Or motherly wholesomeness. Or motherly sexuality. You do understand motherly tenderness and motherly bitterness and motherly care. You understand motherly sacrifice and motherly overwhelm. Motherly exasperation and motherly joy. You understand the big fat food duty and pending outbursts of the improperly fed, the overly tired, the wired-up or disconnected, the greedy little wanting-everything-for-yourself hatefulnesses of family. The untidiness of calling all of this love.

These closenesses that bind children forever in
becoming who they are. Bonds of care, separation,
forgiveness, and co-conspiracy to keep little secrets,
outwit familial harms, create stories of belonging and
unbelonging. Create stories of us—as we are, as we
were, as what we might become given where we came
from. Stories that metastasize recurring narratives
of affect that nonetheless surprise us as we replay
them into being in the everyday. Stories we co-create
unconsciously through the interplay between how we
are made, and what we encounter, and who encounters
us, and how that will later be the work of a lifetime
to unpack and demystify, revealing marvellous and
aberrant truths. The paths we discover and walk upon.
The paths we cut through the underbrush. The paths
we scale along cliff edges. The paths we walk through
grocery stores. The paths we wear in the mind,
shaping our facial cues to correlate us to life.

A peek into Brenda's life:

Brenda scrawls a note into the grocery notebook, trying to
understand why it feels so hard, but the toddler is hungry
and she is hungry so the thought gets left unfinished, as
most of her thoughts do. She eats a bit of toast and slaps on
peanut butter and honey for her and the toddler. She drinks

coffee with cream after the tea has woken her enough that she can muster the courage for these preparations. These things make her feel human. She reads three more books to the toddler in the way toddlers like to read books. A lot of page turning back and forth and book manipulation with some words of great glee and pointed fingers, some complaining and frustration, more glee and surprise that the dog that was there on the page last time doing that silly thing is once again there doing a silly thing after the page has been closed and opened and closed and opened again! Life is full of these hurrah moments. We learn such confidence from books, feeling like if we just look in the right place, the thing that brought us happiness will be there again, waiting, every time we turn the page back to where it was the last time!

It is now six o'clock. Black night becomes blue light. Brenda encounters the dawn with renewed feeling. There will be a day, then another night. Small things will happen. Brenda may encounter them with grace, congratulating herself for remembering to cultivate love, or she may react against them with little fits and tyrannies, replaying past moments of her mother's and father's experienced and inherited overwhelms so that she feels like a rabid thing. All of them will pass, then be repeated. The good times are when the grace bits get repeated most frequently. The hard times are when there is so much hissing from her mouth she must crawl into her shell from the heat in order to regulate herself. It can be hard dwelling in life with all this cold blood. Blood that flares and almost freezes and sometimes feels so cozy warm depending on the temperature of blood of other beings around it.

After scrawling her unfinished thought, Brenda turns the page back and adds cheese to the list for today's groceries.

My Five-Week Course in Ikebana

Lots of people know how to fence, but I'm not one of them. I thought about it once, when I was younger and had extra time to be thinking about trying out new activities. There were a few local rec centres that offered beginner's classes. You could do fencing, or pottery, or ikebana. I took one five-week session of ikebana, from which I took home five bouquets of almost-beautiful-enough-to-be-contemplative bouquets that my boyfriend said were really neat. But he didn't think it would be worth spending the money on the specialized supplies I'd need to really get serious with it as an art form. And what was the point of doing it if I wasn't going to get serious?

I took a few books out from the library and spent a lot of time on Pinterest to get ideas, but I only had the one vase and one spiky frog that I got with the course, and after I had arranged a few stems into the spiky frog in groupings of three — cutting back their stems until they reached harmonious heights relative to one another — I would be left with a bunch of excess greenery and flowers and would end up with these awkward bouquets shoved into Mason jars all over the house.

I tried to put them in spots that would not detract from my ikebana arrangement with their disorder and lack of focused attention, but even if I couldn't see them while I was admiring my ikebana I always knew they were there. I just couldn't bring myself to compost perfectly good materials, and I didn't know how to feel about the haphazard bouquets and the shame they caused me. Because if it hadn't been for the ikebana bouquet, the one I'd been trying for, I think I would have felt happiness seeing those Mason jar bouquets all over the house — little assemblages of colour and scent gifted by the world.

I gave the spiky frog to my friend Marilyn who has quite a few others already. Her ikebana is pretty abstract, and I think a little dark, but she has the money to commission vases from a local potter, and order in botanicals to the florist who specializes in exotic plants, and it keeps her mind off her son Rick, who's been accused of sexually assaulting a young woman he used to go out with. She gets choked up when she starts to talk about it, because she doesn't know how to love her son now that she knows he has done monstrous things. She puts her confusion into the ikebana. I can tell from the way I want to weep when I look at her arrangements. How she makes something so beautiful, and then corrupts it so that it ends up causing you pain somehow when you get close to it.

At the Dentist

The dentist keeps his hair buzzed short. It is all grey and spiky but he is not an old man. Forty-five, maybe, at the most. Probably not that much older than Isabelle, who sits in his chair wearing a red cashmere cardigan and wraparound sunglasses over her eyes with her mouth opened wide, like he told her to. He is okay, as far as dentists go, but because he is a dentist it is really hard to see him as a person. He is doing things to her she does not want him to do: poking at her gums with pointy little tools, making them bleed, dictating words she does not understand about her mouth to his perky two-braided assistant who diligently taps them into a computer with a screen Isabelle cannot see. Files about her dental health she is not allowed to access.

Isabelle is embarrassed about these files. She is embarrassed to have her mouth wide open while a man looks in, assessing her dental housekeeping. She is embarrassed to be wearing black plastic sunglasses that slide down her little nose. Still, she subjects herself to these shameful appointments she has to make a year ahead of time because supposedly these people with their chemicals, tools, and spreadsheets will keep her teeth from rotting out of her skull.

Isabelle sometimes dreams her teeth are falling out and wakes up touching them with her fingers to make sure they are still firmly in place. It is fear that brings her here, fear of what she might become if she is negligent, of the money she might have to spend down the line to stave off the already too-far-gone damages. That one day she may have to resort to skin grafts cultured from her own plasma and the donated flesh of someone the dentist refers to in a casually unproblematic way as a "cadaver." She sits in the chair pretending she is not afraid, as comfortable as it is possible to be in the reclining faux leather with plastic wrap at the bottom where the feet go that probably cost a couple of grand.

The dentist makes little noises like "hmm" and "mhmm" as he pokes and prods with his little mirror. Sometimes he asks her questions that are difficult for her to answer because her mouth has tools in it and feels cakey from the chemicals the hygienist put in before the dentist came by to peer into her cleansed mouth. The dentist waits until after the scraping and polishing to stick his fingers in. Two, maybe three minutes he looks inside, checking on things the hygienist has already noticed and jotted down for him to consider. Then he tells her to have a nice day and goes out of the room and Isabelle goes to the front desk to hand over money to his receptionist.

Perhaps if Isabelle did not have to pay for these abuses that are good for her in the long run she would be more able to accept that the dentist is a person with hopes, dreams, and frustrations just like her. Poor man, she thinks briefly, how must it be for him to see the earnest smiles of people and think of them in terms of stages of decay, rather than absorbing the emanations of simple happiness that pass from human mouth to human soul through the act of baring teeth.

On Alleviating Oneself of Guilt

The little fly on my nightstand puked all over my journal. I was so upset I messaged its mother, but its mother was dead because she had already lived out her long fifteen days on earth by the time I was able to track down her number. Her number had been passed on to one of the fly's hundreds of siblings because it was too confusing and costly for flies to always be signing up for their own phone plans, seeing as they'd never make it through a full billing cycle in one generation.

The fly's sibling never messaged back, so I sent it a photo of its sister's squished body, all mashed up into my white tempered-glass lamp. It was a cruel thing for me to do, but I'm learning to admit that I am often cruel. I want to hurt those who have hurt me. Even though I know so much better, still, the feelings are there.

Afterward I feel guilty for having been an awful person and send a photo of me giving the fly a proper burial. I even hire my neighbour—who used to be a soloist in her church choir—to sing "Amazing Grace" for the fly. I think it's what she would have wanted. That, and the cup of brown sugar I dump right over her body before I scoop the dirt on top. I send a video of the song being sung in the background of the sugar-and-soil ceremony to the fly's sibling to make up for my cruelty, but I'm already too late by the time I edit it down to a clip I can attach via text, because the fly's sibling is dead now too and the number belongs to the fly's nephew, who never knew his aunt and doesn't feel anything like the forgiveness I need to alleviate myself of guilt.

Part Three

Home Breaking

Puff

She eats a moose burger from the last pound she's been saving in the freezer, runs her fingers over the thick sharpie'd letters that spell *Puff*. The last pound of ground from the moose her and Ty shot two seasons ago up the plateau.

They didn't get one this year. Tried but didn't get one. Had a ticket but came home from that trip with no meat. Still, she had been happy to be out there with him. Mostly. Happy and sad at the same time. Because she had known it would be their last trip together, and she really wanted some moose to take home to gran and the kids. Stop rationing out what was left and just eat like there was plenty again. Walk away with plenty. She wanted plenty again. Plenty of everything. Like back when her and Ty first started up, before that first moose, when there was plenty of happiness. For both of them. And her kids could feel that and felt plenty fine.

Not like now, though she keeps holding on to that memory of plenty, hoping it will come back, that empty's just a phase of plenty that is waiting to be filled up again. Now that she knows how empty builds when you're just following along, thinking if you do it right plenty will stay like it's supposed to.

Gran had told her to be careful with Ty because most men don't know themselves enough to be trusted. Gran knew well enough because she'd had her fair share of dealings with men. Men like Ty, and other men too—a couple of sons who looked as white as their fathers, including Alana's papa, and a couple from her first husband, whose skin was as dark as gran's. Gran's white boys and brown boys—all of them not to be trusted. Loved, but not trusted, though god knows gran had given them enough chances. Gran knew for sure how much a woman's love could get her hurt. She also knew how to ration plenty, stretch it out to get her through the lean times.

Alana had listened, as she always listened to gran, but her body didn't want to hear what gran was saying. Her body told her these were different times, and that she was a different woman, that Ty was a different man—that she didn't have to live through the kind of things gran lived through so maybe she could love without feeling so much hurt in it. She already knew enough about how love could hurt, but Alana was young enough to think she had it in her to transform the hurt to something else if she followed the right path.

She remembers the first moose, how it had felt like plenty each time she went to the freezer and took out a piece. How it had been something else first, before it got packaged. Before it became plenty to eat—that first hint of emptiness, though she hadn't known it then. And watching that emptiness spread when she got to the last quarter, when plenty changed for good, when she'd seen real clear that Ty couldn't see enough the things that haunted him to do any kind of healing. And she'd known then there was not much left, but hoped for a while still that there'd be more to fill back what had been eaten up, that they'd get a second moose and make things right somehow. But they hadn't been gifted that and now she was just trying to figure out the best way to walk away without losing too much.

Her moose. The one he'd made her shoot, how she hadn't wanted to, though they'd talked about it first. Talked about how she would be the one to do it. She had thought a lot about how she might feel, prayers she might whisper, ways she might ask, but when the time came, it came with urgency so she couldn't remember the ways she had planned, the crossing words she wanted to whisper to help the animal's spirit pass over, for its body to become meat she could feed her family. She tried pushing the gun away, pleading with him, her liquid brown eyes asking, "Please?" But there was only a hardness looking back. A hardness with a whole lot of judgement in it. Disgust even. That she would become this kind of woman when the time came to do what needed to be done, because it felt dirty or hard or scary, or whatever other feeling it was that felt too big for her to do it. That men always had to be the ones to do the dirty work. That look had scared her then, and it still scares her. Now that she knows these hard places in Ty, the way he turns on her sometimes, making her the enemy. Forgetting everything about her that is good and seeing only her ugliness, like the ways she disappoints him for being weak.

He asked her on that first trip, after they had brought the moose in and she wouldn't come out of the back of the truck, shivering inside her sleeping bag with two layers of wool on her, "Are you just doing this to impress me? 'Cause I ain't impressed. And I don't give a fuck if you hunt. I don't want to have to deal with the hysterics. I don't want to process what you feel about it. You do it or you don't; if you want to cry about it, cry to one of your lady friends. Now we gotta get back and hang this thing so the meat don't spoil. So get the fuck up and help me and stop with the fuck'n tears."

And she had whimpered, "I'm sorry. Sorry Ty," and this snivelling enraged her. She had screamed at him then, a way she hadn't screamed since she was a teenager fighting with her sister over whatever precious resources they felt they needed to hoard from one another. "Fuck you, Ty! I didn't get a chance to learn from my dad like you. Are you too much of a pussy to deal with a woman's tears? Fuck'n coward. I ain't a robot and I won't pretend to be." And this had worn her out completely. Quieter, barely a whisper, to herself more than him, she had said "I'm cold, just so cold. I can't stop shivering."

She could hear him throwing things around in the trailer, packing up, and she had gotten out of her bag, shivering and hot in her head, feeling like her body was as heavy as the dead weight of the carcass they had hauled out. She had peed, looked at the back of him, felt his anger growing out of his spine like sharp hot teeth, then gotten back into the truck and wrapped the bag around her, falling in and out of sleep the twelve-hour drive home. Ty had calmed down enough by the time they pulled up at his house to help her out and into bed. Had taken care of what needed to be done. Had said "You did good, babe, you did real good."

Holding the gun, moose's heart through the sight, what she had whispered was "Forgive me." And after, following the trail of dripping blood into the thick bush, when she saw it there heaving, its breath like thick erratic clouds puffing into the morning's coldness, she thought of Puff the Magic Dragon, how much her kids loved that story. That she had killed Puff and now she and Ty and gran and her kids would eat him. And it made her laugh a bit to think of it. How when they were smaller they liked to joke about what kind of beast they were eating. And now they would be eating Puff. "Thank you," she whispered, looking Puff in the eye, pulling the trigger to send the bullet straight into his brain this time, stop the pain, stop the breathing.

She felt Puff's spirit wash over her, erasing the fear she had felt earlier. Washing her in the immensity of Puff's being. And she had not given a fuck what Ty thought of her when she wept over Puff's body to witness his transition from dragon-moose to meat she would feed her kids with. That gran would show her how to smoke.

He had let her cry for a while, crouched against a birch tree smoking, smell of burnt tobacco mixing with the warm stink of bull moose, frothy bits of grass coagulating at the corners of Puff's lips.

After his smoke, Ty had taken over. She wondered why they called it field dressing when it seemed like a kind of pouring out, stripping and bleeding and cutting — undressing more than anything. He used short syllables and gestures, pointing with his fingers, making mock slices with his knife. "Here, and here," showing her where to cut after they had tied Puff's legs out to nearby trees, splaying him, "Up. Like this." Puff's heavy head uphill from the bottom parts of him.

Ty did not let her handle the knife until the organs had all been removed, the hide as though peeled off — his practised hands making it seem like swimming — gliding the blade to sever membranes, keeping the hide intact for her and gran to tan later in as full a piece as possible. She had read that it would be hard to saw through the animal's bones, but she was surprised at what it felt like in her body, running saw against bone. So unlike wood, that seemed to want to turn itself to dust. She thought of her own spine as she cut, feeling little shards breaking off into her fluid body, things that would later pierce her dreams in sleep, unable to achieve any kind of smooth rhythm. The whole attempt of it feeling like a spectacle of her jaggedness. When Ty took the saw back it looked like nothing, the way his body memory-fitted itself to the moose's bones, breaking them in just the right places, as easy as cracking an egg. "You'll learn," he'd said. "It takes a lot of practice. Moose are hard. Dad didn't let me try with moose 'til I was sixteen. I did deer first, just to try. Learn the feel in my hands. You watch, see how it's done. Try again next time."

It had been so fucking hard, getting Puff out, even cut into quarters, dragging on a makeshift cart cut from young trees, strung together with the rope they'd packed in, covered with a canvas tarp to keep dirt, flies, and wasps off the meat. Not that it was really warm enough for flies and wasps, but they'd find their way to the meat even in cold, Ty told her. They'd hung the pieces they would have to come back for up in a big birch so nothing else could get at them, a bit of a ways away from the entrails. That was what Puff's insides were called now, entrails and offal. Offal wrapped in a bit of red cloth, she had insisted on that — the heart, and kidneys and liver — packed out to feast on later, honouring his life force, the entrails left steaming there in a pile where Puff had lain down. Where she'd shot him the second time. The bits of Puff's spirit still in her weren't angry though, just curious. A strange thing to be regarding one's insides on the outside of oneself, felt the thing in her. She sensed that. The spirit bits didn't feel the same way about the chunks of muscle and bone she was hauling, not that way about the meat. It was the entrails that made them feel that way.

By the time they'd hauled out the first two quarters it was almost dark. She didn't think she could summon the strength to do it, haul out the other two. Knowing the last would be in pitch-blackness. She was wet with sweat, even in her wool; each time they stopped it cooled her to freezing. They had walked farther in from the truck than planned, and the ground was rough, though the trail was getting smoother each time they passed the cart over. Still lots of brush, and wet. She was fucking cold. She had read online that some people did that, hauled out what they could, then came back the next day. So she'd asked. But that's not the way Ty did things. Not the way his dad did them. "We gotta do it, just two more hours, that's it, then we can drive back to camp. You're gonna hurt tomorrow either way, it won't be any easier coming back up and doing it then. Faster we can get it out, the better. Less to worry about."

It had been four hours, because of how fucking slow she was going, Ty told her. And afterwards, back home, it had taken her weeks to warm up. Halfway out on the last quarter her legs had given out, her whole body shaking.

Ty had been gentle at first, encouraging, then screamed at her to get the fuck up 'cause there was no way in fucking hell he was going to drag this out and come back to haul her ass out too. He had grabbed her arm and pulled her up, shaken her and tossed her back down, said he'd drag the fucking cart himself but she had to walk herself out or he was leaving her.

Lying in bed shivering, tracing the line of welts, the blue-and-yellow trace of his fingers on her skin. Fingers that until Puff had made her feel only pleasure. She remembers getting up, following, following. Saying to herself over and over again, "Following Ty, following Ty, following Ty."

The Pregnancy Test

Gloria takes a pregnancy test in the Skeena Mall then stuffs the package into the tampon bin leaving half the box sticking out. Five women use the stall after her and before Layla starts her evening cleaning shift and dumps the bin into the rolling wastebasket she takes to the dumpster out back.

Layla pulls the box out with her blue latex gloves because the bin is overflowing and she can't pull the bag out without spilling the contents unless she takes the box out first. She shakes the box and finds it empty, peers into the bin to see if it's been dropped inside, but the wand is nowhere to be found. Layla wonders what happened to the magic stick and hopes to hell whoever took the test didn't flush it because that will be a romping mess to clean later when the toilet gets plugged up.

Of the five women who use the stall after Gloria, all but one are tempted to pull the wand out of the box and see the results, but only Meeru and Iris do. Iris hesitates, because of the ickiness factor, but she's been waiting to see a positive on one of these sticks for three years now so she can't stop the compulsion to look, thinking maybe, just maybe, this is the omen she's been waiting for. If this one shows a plus sign, maybe her next one will too?

~

Tanis looks at the box for a long time and wonders about the girl who took it. She tries to piece together the girl's story. Tanis assumes that it was a girl because a woman would most likely take the thing home, not have to hide in a dingy stall in the mall. Unless it was a woman who was hoping and really wanted to know and couldn't wait? But wouldn't a woman like that put the box somewhere less visible? Wouldn't she take it out to the big wastebasket instead of jamming into the tampon bin and creating an inconvenience to all the other women with sanitary pads and tampon applicators who would use the toilet after her? Tanis assumes that only a girl could be so hasty, a girl in some kind of trouble. *Poor girl*, she thinks. *I hope it was a minus sign.*

Tanis pretends she isn't tempted to actually check the applicator, but she is. Like Iris, the thought of a stranger's secretions is a barrier to her curiosity. Unlike Iris she is not hoping for a plus sign. It would be an absurdist nightmare, singularly impossible outside of immaculate conception for Tanis to ever see a plus sign, since she went through menopause over two decades ago and hasn't had sex with a man in over forty years. And thank God for that! Tanis can satiate her curiosity by other means.

She sits on the toilet remembering the last member to slime its way inside her, like a blind mole pushing and poking its way underground. *Thank God. At least cocks don't have little scratching claws to dig their way into us!* She chuckles a little bit to think of men's penises snuffling along dark passageways with little furry claws sticking out of them that come to life with an erection. Otherwise dangly little things that kick into gear when the blood swells, poking and digging this way and that. *Oh!* she thinks. *As if women don't have enough to worry about without getting all scratched up on top of it!* She chuckles all the way to the sink, where she gives her hands a good wash, humming her ABCs while she scrubs the backs and fronts and in-betweens to make sure she wipes off any vaginal bacteria, cold viruses, or flu bugs picked up from the public washroom.

The woman in the next stall over halts mid-pee when she hears Tanis chuckling. Then she hears Tanis humming at the sink and realizes it's just an old woman who sings and laughs and probably talks to herself. Still, she can't finish her business until the old coot shuffles out the door.

〜

Meeru pinches two pieces of toilet paper between her fingers to pull the wand out. She doesn't want to touch it because she knows there's someone's pee all over it, seeing as it's pretty much impossible to hold the wand under the stream without it splashing all over. She'll wash her hands for an extra minute afterwards, once she's found out how the coin toss turned out today for whoever left this mystery for Meeru to figure out.

Meeru works in the jewellery shop kitty-corner to the bathroom corridor and the day has been slow. She's seen just about every woman who has come in and out of the bathroom, most of them familiar faces. In winter the mall is pretty much the only place to go to get out of the weather. Meeru is a close observer of people. She has to be to make her sales, to help people pick out their wedding rings and mementoes. She has to develop a deep understanding of how to counsel customers so that they are able to turn little pieces of metal and rock mined from the earth in mostly inhumane and ecologically devastating ways into symbols of lasting intimacy. Meeru's vocation is to tease out the bonds of love latent in these small glittery things. Our own pieces of the stars, Meeru thinks. She gets it because she comes from a long line of jewellers, though she's only been once to see her grandfather's shop back in her mother's home country. She takes pride in what she does, and despite the aesthetic inclinations of her customers in this small town, who favour gaudy, pedestrian gems, Meeru does her best to convince the owner to order good-quality stones, and popular styles that are as artful as possible.

Meeru looks forward to the day when she owns this business, or if not this one, then another—when she'll be able to source the most ethical rocks and metals possible (though she doubts any of the mall clientele could afford them). She daydreams of a boutique in Vancouver where the kind of wealthy people she's never met might wander in for a meaningful consultation, with enough extra money not just to buy beauty, but to care about where it comes from. Meeru won't ask them where their investments lie, because she's pretty sure that behind the ethical purchases and compassionate displays of wealth there will be capital that does a heck of a lot more harm somewhere else than the good it claims to do with its guilt-free jewellery.

Meeru runs back through the list of faces who walked down the lavatory hall today as she pulls the wand out. She picks out seven women or girls of childbearing age who had intense or furtive looks to them. Perhaps all, but at least one of them, plagued by the anxious secrets of ovulation.

Aisla hasn't slept for more than forty-five minutes in a row for over a year. She looks at her list again sitting on the toilet, the baby sleeping in the bucket seat on the floor, one of her feet rocking as she tries to pee without splashing all over the toilet and her pants. Have to keep rocking or he'll wake up and getting him to sleep takes up so much of her life that any respite when he actually is sleeping is heavily and anxiously guarded. She has to look at her list again because she forgets something every time. She knows she's forgotten to write things on her list, but the most important things are probably on there. Probably. It's a fifty-two-minute drive into town, and if she's lucky he'll fall asleep halfway and stay asleep for twenty minutes after — enough time for her to grab a coffee at the Tim Hortons drive-thru and take a pee in the mall bathroom before she starts her errands.

The moving car or the swinging seat are the only places he'll sleep long stretches. She has to be so slow stopping, so quiet opening the doors, and so fast and smooth pulling him out so she doesn't wake him, dreading every second that she'll fuck up or something will fuck her up and he'll wake, wailing, another epic fail of a trip to town, him fussing the whole time, needing to nap again before she's got half her list done.

Today Aisla is lucky. He's asleep and her aim is good. Her muscles honed for the one-legged pee. Aisla looks up from her list and sees the box. She sees it but doesn't feel anything. Aisla feels very little other than tiredness, anxiety, and rage these days. The other thing she thinks she feels is love for her baby. Deep, exasperated love. But it isn't like other kinds of love that have parts of herself in them. Love in which she is reflected back to herself, in which she is revealed somehow, or the world is revealed to her. What she feels for the baby has no revelation of herself in it. It has nothing to do with who she is and everything to do with how she was made. Her design is revealed to her through it, but she doesn't get to choose its expression, just has to ride along. She thought before that would be the wonder of it, the riding along. Didn't realize there'd be so many bumps and scratches, that she'd be doing most of it alone. That it would be like a year of ongoing turbulence mid-flight over the Pacific with no end in sight. Not like the motherhood story she had in her head, a soft tender journey nestled in outpourings of maternal love.

She remembers longing for it before she had it. Or at least longing for the idea of it. She thought it would have something to do with the full realization of her body, but she thinks now maybe this was a trick. It takes from her body without giving back. Feeding and sucking and growing. She's read it described as parasitic. The body wanted this and did not know what it was getting into. Went through it all without her mind, once it all got started and she decided to invite the semen in.

She remembers buying a two-pack pregnancy test, and the disappointment when the first one came up with just one line instead of two. It wasn't the plus or minus kind like this one. But the second one she took, the one that must have ended up showing two lines, she doesn't remember taking. Or what she did with the box. Or the wand. In a landfill somewhere, she guesses. The box burned or recycled. She would have taken it at home. Did she show him or just tell him? Did he even know about the test? Did she tell him soon after or did she wait? Wait for a moment when it seemed he would share something with her? Share what? What did she feel when the second line came up? She doesn't remember that either. Maybe that was when all the forgetting began? Maybe all the forgetting has something to do with all the other losses now that everything is so full of baby?

The baby stirs and Aisla whispers "fuck" under her breath. She stands up without wiping and swings a little more until he settles again, then grabs and rips one handed, dabs a thick swab of toilet paper as quickly as she can, shimmies, and pulls up her panties, then leggings. They bunch but she'll have to live with it for now. She's learned not to wear anything to town that has buttons or zippers, because of this dance in the bathroom. Because of the sleep. Aisla looks at the box again and is overcome with an urge to rip the box to shreds and stomp the fucking stick over and over and over again. Do violence unto the stick and all the promises and terrors it represents in its perky white-and-pink box. All the secrecy.

Then Aisla sobs. Big heaving sobs. Her sobs wake the

baby and the baby wails. Her sobs change to coos and she takes it out of its seat with such tenderness. She dances and whispers, "Mama's here, mama's here, shhh, it's okay." Then she sits and pulls up her shirt and is flooded by warmth when the baby latches. They are both soothed by the letdown, ensconced in the pleasure of closeness. Aisla softens toward the box and is able to think outside of all the immediacies while the baby feeds. She doesn't think about the public washroom and all of her mother's warnings as a child not to touch anything. She doesn't even register the smell of the antiseptic soap and bleach residue. What she feels is a visceral flush of empathy for the woman. The woman who put the box here. A real woman in the world walking around with relief or great happiness, perplexing ambiguity or abject terror, curiosity or bewilderment. Aisla takes some deep breaths into the feeling and watches it expand and move like a light outside of her, toward someone out in the world. Outside of her and the baby.

When the baby is done it beams at her. She flushes then and the baby laughs. Aisla says goodbye to the box and goes out into the mall to find a shopping cart in which to push the baby and all the heavy things the baby needs.

⁓

Darcy is just a little bit fucked-up when she gets into the stall and locks the door behind her. She managed to make it in without the fake cops seeing her and harassing her to get out of the mall, dragging her by the arm if she puts up a fuss. Or if it's the nice one, walking with her and standing outside the door until she pisses and comes out, threatening to come in and get her if she takes too long. She's just going to get warm for a bit, sit quietly without her arse hanging out in the cold behind a dumpster or in the park hoping no one's going to see her or that she doesn't get it all over her shoes and pants because she doesn't have any others to change into. Pee smell lingering in her panties because she doesn't have any toilet paper to wipe up with. And it's too cold today to get wet and hang her butt out there. She pictures the pee freezing on its way out, yellow icicles hanging from her pubic hair. She'll wait in here as long as she can—if she's lucky, long enough to get everything she needs to do done before they find her out. Things are spinning a bit, but not too much. And the stall wall is a good place to rest her head. She even sleeps a little, which is a blessing. Darcy is tired. She's been tired for months. And it feels safe in here for now, preternaturally quiet.

She hadn't noticed it before, but when she opens her eyes, Darcy sees the box. First thought is *poor fucking thing*. It hurts to see the box. She thinks of her babies and wonders what they're doing, what they look like now. It's been two years since she's seen them. Not babies anymore. She tries not to think about them most of the time. When she does it's the good she remembers, the good she did, and not all the other shit. The mama she was. The mama she is. "My babies," she says, when she's talking to the other girls on the street and they talk about their own. The pride they get to share when they talk about their babies, the good things they brought into the world. How all the good things get taken away.

She knows she's coming down because the things she doesn't want to think about are coming back. How she swore she'd do better than had been done to her. All the ways she tried to do better but it all got fucked-up and she can't pinpoint how or when or why. It all just adds up, all the fucked-up shit, no matter how hard she tries. The babies that wouldn't know her now, even though she gave so much to them. She's really coming down because she also thinks of the two abortions. Her drain babies.

They give her a shot now, and she hasn't had a scare in a while. Hasn't bled in a while either. She's skinny now, too skinny to bleed, or maybe it's the shot that does that? She isn't sure but she thinks they said something about that when they talked about side effects.

Darcy is about to pull the box out of the bin when the security guard comes in and bangs on the stall door. "I know you're in there, Darce, time's up."

Fucking Craig must've told her to come check to make sure she wasn't OD'ing again. He's the one keeps bringing in stronger and stronger stuff, not that she minds the knockout high, but she's so tired, tired of watching her friends twitch past the good into the gnarly, knowing the next hit might kill you.

She just wanted enough time to hide the fucking box. Bury it deep in the paper towel bin so its spell wouldn't catch anyone else. Put it to rest somehow.

Erosion

Her lips are chafed up, they've been around so many cocks
by now, bits of her lip skin left behind on the shaft when
it retreats back down, tucked into foreskins until johns or
boyfriends scrub them off, dripping down innumerable
drains over the years, decaying amongst the skin cells of
the men who provide. She prefers the uncircumcised ones,
how much easier it slides, less work needed, less spit and
lube. For the ones that pay extra not to wear a condom, or
the boyfriends that won't. Sometimes, depending on how
much, she'll suck naked cock for a stranger, though she says
she doesn't. She hates the taste of latex, thinks maybe it's
the latex that irritates her lips, or the fact she's never liked
water. Used to only drink it with lemon or cucumber in it,
now can't afford to get a hold of those things, has to drink
it plain, so doesn't, prefers the watered-down coffee she
gets from the shelters.

She's too messed up to make good coin on cock like some of the other girls do. Not a girl anymore. It isn't a steady job, just something she does when she needs to get a hit and she doesn't have a boyfriend who supplies it for her.

Her lips feel like cracked pastry, flaking away into air. When she blows her breath out into the cold, some of her parts blow away. She wishes her whole body could float away, settle onto the ocean, be eaten up by crustaceans, transformed into shell that will crumble to sand when the animal dies and its hard exterior is crushed beneath the ocean's weight. Thousands of years later washed ashore and baked in a tropical sun. After all the humans are gone and there are no more cocks to suck, just simpler beasts who fuck to make more of themselves, or bud children from their mixed-sex bodies. Her bones will be crushed beneath layers of dust from all the decaying cities, all the flesh of her sisters and children long consumed by things that scurry.

It will be so peaceful. There will be no more need then, or guilt or shame, everything left of her moved about by wind or water, the shifting dance of earth.

Merry Christmas

The bed Connie lies in is hopeful and dirty. It is made from the holiday cloth of all the Christmases she lived in another life. The life before this one. The warm life in which she was part of a family and maybe even happy there. She had a bed then, and linens. A linen closet that she complained was too full. Too many linens, even. Now she's lucky if she has a blanket. A warm blanket.

Tonight she has a minus-forty-Celsius-rated sleeping bag that she traded Bissie for because Bissie's got a spot at the shelter and Connie had lifted a Coral Bliss lipstick Bissie wanted. Bissie said she'll want the bag back when she's out on the street again, but she knows Connie might not have it by then. Someone else might end up with it for a while because it's a damn good bag and nothing to waste. It will get stashed somewhere eventually though, and it might take a while, but Bissie will find it again if she asks around and has something good to swap for it. It will probably get swiped at the shelter anyway, so it may as well keep Connie warm for some nights, since it's Christmas and there's not enough room at the shelter and it's under freezing all this week.

Hard to hold on to things for very long when you've got nowhere to keep them, things make the rounds, sometimes you see them again, sometimes you don't, and if you're lucky you get something for them in exchange.

Connie is warm, even though the bag stinks like other people's sweat and sex. For her pillow she uses the sweater she sews bits of cloth into, the only thing she's managed to keep with her all these years. Four swatches, one for each of her babies, the only thing she has of them. Not even any pictures, just four scraps of cloth from pieces of clothes they wore five years ago, the last time she saw them. Five Christmases ago. Bits of their Christmas pyjamas. The ones grandma used to send to them every year when Connie had an address to send things to. Maybe grandma still sends pyjamas to their new addresses? Addresses Connie doesn't know because if she did she might show up there wasted and try to see them or take things that don't belong to her from the people she loves. She might bring one of her boyfriends with her to threaten their father if he didn't let her see them, or one of her girlfriends to help her plead for just one hug, depending on what she was on.

Connie doesn't think it's stealing if you take things from

the people you love. Even if you don't ask, even if they wouldn't give it to you if you did. Because Connie gave everything to the people she loved. So much giving that a big chaos of emptiness grew in her where all the love had been. It hurt, that chaos, still hurts, but it's hopeful tonight because Connie's got a warm bed and warm memories and her body is full of heroin and that fills the emptiness so full all the cold gnawing chaos sleeps for a little while.

She's having a *merry* Christmas.

Connie drifts into sleep, the coziness wrapped around her.

Heroin wears off though, taking with it her fullness. If she could, she'd be on it forever.

She wakes thinking of how the people she loves have so much while she has nothing now. They have more than enough to give to her, even if they keep it locked behind closed doors and they changed the keys from when she used to be allowed in to shower and do laundry, and they don't even invite her in anymore to warm up for a little while or eat something, because every time they do, something goes missing.

Connie doesn't think it hurts them as much as it does when she takes and takes and takes until no one wants to give anymore. It's been a long time since she cared about how the people she loves feel about her, or how they feel at all. She knows they'll be okay; they'll get over it. And besides, their whirlwind of needs and wants mean nothing to her the way they once did when she had needs and wants that matched theirs and could live in relationship with them. When she used to be able to listen to what other people talked about and register it somewhere in herself, being moved to tend back in the ways she was being tended. There are so many other basic things she has to care about now. So much time spent figuring out where her next hit is coming from. When you have nothing you have to craft your way into things to get the only thing that you really want. It takes everything.

Ropes of Entropy

Deep in the mountains, in a hospital in an abandoned town, John Handy is born with a beautiful set of fox ears and Josh Outage is not. The hospital is one of the few scattered buildings left now that the Company has moved the residents fifteen kilometres upriver — because living among the slag heaps with all that dust has been deemed detrimental to employee longevity.

John Handy grows up thinking the world of himself. He believes he is meant for greatness. He believes not only that he is meant for greatness, but also, more brazenly, that he is the central existential axis upon which the entire world depends. Would the world even exist, John wonders, if I did not exist? He thinks that it would not. He writes notes to his best friend, Josh, and attaches them with clothespins to the pulley that stretches from his window in #13 to Josh's window in #14, stretching the twenty feet across the yard that separates their trailers. The notes say things like, *Yer mom smelz like dog farts.*

Josh thinks the world of John. He keeps the notes John passes in a special box under his bed. Even when they're mean, which they usually are. Every once in a while he'll get something that shows the better parts of John, saying something like, *Best part of wintr is erly nite, i can see in yer window.*

Josh sends back notes that John doesn't keep—little things like, *Do you think the stars can see in too?*

John doesn't answer Josh's questions, stops writing back, or just sends the next thing that pops in his mind to say. He thinks a lot about animal dicks and gets Josh to answer whose dick he thinks is bigger. Josh has a whole series of these:

mouse or shrue?

Hors or elk?

Weezel or musckrat?

Despite John's lack of interest in Josh, their friendship flourishes. Josh is devoted to John because John embodies the kind of masculinity Josh wishes for himself. John is unflinchingly confident, even though his confidence has no basis to it. John is not, after all, accomplished in anything other than his own opinion of himself. He is neither generous nor kind, has no special skills, is unremarkable looking—other than his beautiful silver fox ears—and is of mediocre intelligence, able to grasp concepts but not to generate any kind of original or creative extension of these concepts beyond the contexts to which they are routinely applied. John Handy thinks only and always primarily of himself, and expects others to do so also.

Josh has admired John's ears for as long as he can remember, growing up right next door to his magnificent friend in the Company trailer park hastily put down alongside the tracks during the coal boom of '78 when so many families moved to town they had to raze the cottonwoods along the river and the pines on the upper bank to lay out as many homes as possible in the shortest amount of time. Seven trailer parks in all went up between '78 and '84 with names like Mountain View, Engelmann Spruce Court, Pine Estates, and Cottonwood Acres.

You'd think that the fox ears might have made John an outcast, but folks were used to little bits of strangeness up there in the mountains. Mrs. Henlie, for instance, with the silky mouse whiskers growing out the sides of her nose, and Gavin Faraccone with the skin lesions like impressionist flowers all up his arms and neck right up to his temples — such a beautiful flourishing one became lost looking at him in profile. Mandy with the extra foot growing sideways out of her left ankle, with that toddle walk that marked her from a good ways off, and Sheila Powers with the goat-beard hair.

Before it was this town, it had been three other ragtag towns, side by side along the creek, each town close enough to the different holes cut into the mountain that the men could walk directly into the earth from home. Towns where people hauled away the earth's black insides on the iron horse — a gathering of shacks and shops between two mountains where long ago underground seams caught fire and, half a century later, parts of the mountain are still burning. So people expect a bit of strangeness now and then, and don't make much of a fuss about it when it turns up. They just keep hoping the Company will pay, that it will be boom rather than bust when it's time to sign a new contract so they won't lose out much, so they'll be able to pay the mortgage and the truck payments, and so they can buy that new sled for little Ricky, who has outgrown the junior model, take the family on a cruise next winter after the hunting season is over.

So the ears, although odd, are not necessarily remarkable. Josh thinks the ears let John hear things in the world that other people can't, that they give him superpowers other folks don't have. And they should. That was the intention of them. That was what Mrs. Handy had hoped when she took fox form the night of John's conception. But although beautiful, the ears do not work on John Handy the way they might work on a boy with more openness to magic. Josh, really, is the one blessed with curiosity about the world. He wonders about how creatures other than himself might experience being who and what they are. He is curious about John's difference and how this leads him to be who he is. He thinks John is beautiful, even though most of the other kids think he's a run-of-the-mill bully.

John is bigger than the other boys and although pudgy, you wouldn't call him fat. He doesn't do dismally in school and doesn't lip off to the teachers. Among adults he commands very little attention, but in a middling way that only other boys know about, John pushes them around. None more so than Josh, who bears the brunt of John's posturing. Josh is special to John because of his loyalty. John knows that he'll take whatever he gives with an underdog's fierce devotion. Lucky for John Handy to have a friend like Josh. A friend who will stay with him beyond boyhood, wanting to be near him always.

When they were young they spent a lot of time doing bad things that John would suggest and Josh would go along with. John mostly got his ideas from television shows he watched, and books he read about how boys used to be, back before parents were always keeping a close eye on them, putting them in all sorts of organized activities and making them stay indoors the rest of the time, so as to keep them safe.

John used to steal cigarettes from his chain-smoking mom for him and Josh to smoke down at the river. They'd go through a pack in an hour, smoking cig after cig, not really inhaling but pretending they were, because they had to smoke the whole pack before getting home so their parents wouldn't find out about it. They built a little shelter just above the flood line where they stashed things they deemed important to their wilderness activities. It was just a hole in the ground covered with branches and rocks, nowhere near waterproof, so they couldn't keep their cigarettes in there without getting them damp. But they did have lighters and wooden matches in plastic baggies that they used for the fires they liked to light, a couple of knives filched from the hunting gear Josh's dad, Carl, left behind when he went for a motorbike trip down to Sturgis and didn't bother coming back, some fishing tackle, and a glass jar they were saving up coins in for running away to find Josh's dad.

When they couldn't get cigarettes they tried to smoke other things — grasses and pond reeds, bits of moss and lichen. And there was the one time John dared Josh to smoke a dried coyote turd that made him puke his guts out, but not before burning his lips to blisters when the rabbit hairs ignited, singing his mouth instantaneously.

"Hey Josh, give me the last drag of the cigarette, you fuck'n pussy. You smoke like such a cunt."

"Whatever, man, if I smoke like a cunt then you smoke like you're sucking on yer mom's dildo. Seems like you don't even inhale half the time."

"Come 'ere and say that, you fuck."

"Oww, fuck off, John! That fuck'n hurts, stop, stop. Okay, I'm sorry, I shouldn't have said shit about your mom. Seriously, stop, stop yer bein' a fuck'n douchebag."

"Yer the one wants to suck dick. You want ass so much you can smoke this hairy piece of shit to show you're sorry."

"Fuck off, Handy, I'm not gonna smoke shit. Seriously, man, get off, I'm sorry. Yer gonna break my fuck'n leg."

"I'll get off if you promise to smoke the shit, stop crying like a fuck'n pussy and smoke it. Show you're not a fag. I fuck'n dare you. Then you'll know what happens if you ever say shit about my mom again."

"Oww! Fuck! Fuck'n asshole! Shit! My fuck'n lips! Fuck, Fuck!"

"Man, that's sick! Get some water on them. You're such a fuckhead, Outage!"

Josh told his mom he bit into a charred hot dog too soon out of the fire but she couldn't get over the fact that he smelled like burnt shit until his lips finally healed over. For years Vicky refused to let him eat hot dogs.

～

Now that they are both nearing thirty-five, John and Josh spend a lot less time together. They both have jobs and mortgages to pay on overpriced condos in Vancouver. John spends a good amount of time travelling to install accounting software for a national financial corporation and Josh does video game design for a small start-up downtown. It's been a couple of decades since John had his ears done. Cut the whole getup off and built new ones up from scratch with donated cartilage and skin grafted off his backside. Worked with some hotshot plastic surgeon who had spent time doing prosthetics for sci-fi films before turning to medicine, who was used to working with folks like John. A doctor who thought of himself as a sculptor for clients who had parts attached that they later wanted removed when their lovers or lives changed and they no longer wanted a raccoon tail or orangutan-fur pubic hair.

For a while John kept both his original ears in a black leather pouch that his mother made for him. When he moved out he hung the pouch from his bathroom mirror— a spot where his pouch has been strung in each of his various apartments to remind him of the remarkableness he was born with, even if he found living in the world easier without a full set of fox ears framing his otherwise ordinary face. John has not looked in the pouch since they were teenagers, so he doesn't know that for over a decade there has been only the left shrivelled-up, silver-furred ear in there—the right stored in an identical leather pouch hidden safely away in Josh's night table, the extra bulk in John's bag made up by a piece of fox-ear-sized coyote pelt.

Josh hadn't known ahead of time that John was going to have the ears removed, because John didn't tell him. John had just said he was going to be gone over summer vacation and was vague about where. Josh had imagined a summer of nakedness down at the river, wrestling in the water, sunning themselves like otters, stroking one another's cocks with hard fists and pretending after it was just this one time until the next time happened—their last summer together before adolescence—just twelve-year-old-boys being boys, before they would be expected to get summer jobs and girlfriends and plan for futures neither could imagine if they didn't contain mutant superpowers and badass guns.

"I don't know, man, I don't fuck'n know where my mom is taking me. Some shit-ass place to visit some shit-ass friend of hers I don't even know. It's going to be so fuck'n boring."

"That fuck'n sucks, John, it's gonna blow balls here without you around. Hey, you wanna take my Hulk comics with you and I can keep your X-Men? Then we can trade back when you get home?"

Two weeks later, John walked into Josh's room with the stack of Hulk comics, and Josh did not recognize him. He looked at the comics and up at John's face, back down at the comics and his eyes landed on John's eyes, his boy's heart-mind having to rearrange all sorts of felt truths enough that he could speak to the new boy in front of him. The boy without the fox ears. His heart seeing the boy with the fox ears whom Josh loved, and his eyes seeing this new regular boy holding his Hulk comics, speaking in John's voice.

"Hey man, Hulk is sick, you were right. What did you think of the X-Men?"

"The fuck, John?"

"Yeah, I know, yeah. But I still don't get how it works

with the green Hulk and the grey Hulk. Do you have the ones that spell that shit out?"

When John had first had them removed, he and Josh would look at them from time to time to check out the stages of desiccation. Mrs. Handy had salted and tanned the ears after John had them removed, sewed and beaded a pouch to hold them, tucked in other medicines. She hoped they might hold their power until John was ready to understand the gift she had given him. John and Josh took out the bits of cedar and smoked the tobacco. When they were fourteen they started keeping their bud in there, the only kind of medicine they were interested in, and John lost interest in the ears altogether.

"Hey man, I got some of Faraccone's bud this week when I helped with an irrigation ditch out over at his place."

"Sweet, Outage, let's smoke that shit."

"Not tonight, man, we've got a math test tomorrow and I still gotta study; let's save it for this weekend. My mom's got a date Friday night and said I could rent a game. We can get high and play *Mortal Kombat*. But we gotta keep it here 'til then, you know how my mom's always sniffing everything I take home."

"Yeah, man, yeah, my mom smokes so much she can't smell shit. We'll just put it in the medicine bag," said John with a wry grin, pulling down the ear pouch.

Josh felt something in him vibrate every time he thought of the pouch. Knowing their dope would wait for them

with the ears until Friday, all bound up with Mrs. Handy's
magics, gave Josh wet dreams all week long.

"That's fuck'n hilarious, Handy. Medicine bag, fuck."

It became routine for Josh to drop whatever he got trad-
ing Faraccone for odd jobs into the ear bag and every time
he did, he got the inkling to take one of the ears out and take
it home. Josh knew John never took out the ears anymore,
just fished in there for the little baggies Josh would put in.
Josh cut a piece of coyote pelt off one of the hides down in
the field by the river where Mr. Henlie was always putting
them after he shot and skinned them, thinking it would be a
warning to the other coyotes not to come back. They came
back anyway, but Mr. Henlie was always telling anyone
who'd listen that this was the best way to deal with coyotes.
"Send them a message they could understand."

Josh stole the ear because he had always wanted it for
himself, and because it was difficult for him to keep loving
John as tenderly when he started going around in the world
like an ordinary boy acting out dominant tendencies on his
mild-mannered friend. The ear reminded Josh of all the
marvellous things in the world that are hard to grasp with
the mind, bits of spontaneous beauty crashing all around us
that cannot be guessed at, joys of childhood discovery that
need no reason, giving rise to a world full of curiosity and
danger. Josh revered the ear—by taking it he was finally
able to have some of its magic for himself, and by treasuring
it he was able to keep up his profound love for John Handy.

Every night for the last fifteen years Josh has stroked the ear softly, asking for a good stream of dreams, so now if you were to compare the two ears, you'd be hard pressed to make a match. John's ear is a bit mangy, with patches worn off where moths got at it, the silver washed out to a dull grey. Josh's ear, however, is glossy — a resplendent argent that tickles the fingers, awakening a primal sensation of warm nuzzles.

⌒

John Handy and Josh Outage's practices of friendship have shifted since childhood. Instead of spending time together thinking up gross things to make one another laugh, or finding ways to touch each other's bodies, Josh and John exchange texts. Josh, a man of few words, mostly texts John photos of things he knows John will find amusing. Things like exploded ketchup packets under a waitress's shoe at a family diner, or blood pooling out of the plastic wrap of the too-warm meat at the corner grocery, crusts of laundry powder in the old top loaders at the laundromat, and the rainbow of gum wads underneath the table at the fried chicken place. John, a man who thinks the world is made better by the presence of his thoughts in it, texts back opinion pieces. Usually just snippets about what he thinks of the urinals at Starbucks *(some sick shit)*, exclamations about the latest episode of *Game of Thrones*

(Fuck yeah, I'd ride that dragon!), ratings of his most recent meal *(Steak with dollop of blue cheese butter & truffle frites at Moulin 7/10)*, or getting caught behind a mom buying a week's worth of groceries with two toddlers in her cart when he's picking up a pack of Tic Tacs for tonight's date:

> The fuck is it with the plastic car carts at safeway
> MILF knocked over whole stack of oreos near checkout two
> toddlers scarf cookies
> stuck in line for 20 mins
> nice view of lululemons from behind tho ;)

In the last few years something has shifted and John has started to get more philosophical. He writes longer exposés whose meanings are often obscured by the auto-fill on his phone that he doesn't bother to check before sending.

Josh saves the treatises John texts him, the same way he used to save John's misspelled notes as a boy. He enjoys deciphering the intended meaning, believing that some-where between the intended and the unintended exists the true wonder of John. In Josh's mind, the erroneous dupli-cation exists because of John's fallible beauty, his brilliance that is always contradicted by a laziness and lack of rigour, an attention that is not quite there.

Because Josh is sentimental he takes the time to type up and print his favourite interpretations on crepe paper that

he frames and tacks up in his bathroom, reminding him of
John as he washes and empties himself.

Ropes on enter bind me to all
my fevered enterprises. Yet I
preserving, creating systems
to account for Eve aspect of
my being. Each Inchon of time
seeming - to cog around the
particular substrate of Matt
that manifests as me.

Ropes of entropy bind me to
all my fevered enterprises. Yet
I persevere, creating systems
to account for every aspect of
my being. Each inching of time
seaming—to cohere around the
particular substrate of matter
that manifests as me.

Without systems what am I
but another's loft? Another left
turning behind as seen from
the viewpoint of an idle womb
wringing her hands on a sidewalk bench?

Without systems what am I but
another loafer? Another
left-turning vehicle as seen from
the viewpoint of an idle woman
wringing her hands on a sidewalk bench?

What am I but a trim of longing? wanting with all my
existence to sea that which
does not convo to my author-
ship of life. Here I am! Pros
that all the work was bro into
bed only to make me.

What am I but a truncheon of
longing? Wanting with all my
existence to smash that which
does not conform to my author-
ship of life. Here I am! Proof
that all the world was brought
into being only to make me.

If you looked carefully through Josh's records, reading
through the ones stashed in the box under his bed alongside
the ones he's spent time deciphering and typing up, you

would notice that John's depression started around the time he turned thirty. At first it was just a bout here and there of low feelings, something he could kick out of by starting up a new jogging routine, doctoring his dating profile to land more exotic women, or taking a trip over to Thailand where his white skin and Western cash could buy him all sorts of string-free goodies. Then the lows became habit, bolstered by a healthy appetite for blazing that layered social paranoia on top of an ego that had become more and more fragile with years of not being recognized for the wonder of a man that he was.

Smooth about me is shifts. I have always been all. The war shot have ember me as a hero but instead I cut my fucking ears off and what has it got me? A bunch of use pawns who don't undress the cyst I set up for them to make their lives easy. They can't figs out the simple common and who is blamed for their failures? This is the way things were meant to be.	Something about me is shifting. I have always been alone. The world should have embraced me as a hero but instead I cut my fucking ears off and what has it gotten me? A bunch of useless pawns who don't understand the systems I set up for them to make their lives easier. They can't figure out the simplest commands and who is blamed for their failures? This isn't the way things were meant to be.

From thirty-three onward, with a few exceptions when John was feeling untenably hopeful, John's texts shifted from self-aggrandizing to bleak. After John started sending texts that hinted at suicide Josh decided it was time to open up the money jar he'd fished out from their hiding place when he went off after graduation.

When I go it will be like a star burnt out, cost shut off.	When I go it will be like a star burning out, cosmic shutoff.

Though John had stopped putting money in when they went to high school and time down at the river became time in the basement smoking dope and playing video games, Josh put a cut of his gas station wage into that jar all through their teenage years. Even during university when he was accruing student debt and eating off his tips from the coffee shop, Josh put a little something in every month. The last several years it had been a lot more, and by now the jar had expanded into a bank account that held thirty-three grand.

Josh bought them matching 2008 Heritage Softail Classics—Josh's with orange detailing and John's straight black. He signed them up for motorcycle lessons and told John it was finally time they head down to Sturgis to see if they could find out anything about his dad.

John was reluctant, said he couldn't get the time off work. "Get real, Outage, how fuck'n likely is it we're going to learn anything about a man who disappeared willingly more than two decades ago?"

But Josh was unusually persistent. "C'mon, John, it'll be

an adventure. We used to talk about it all the time. We aren't getting any younger, why don't we just fuck'n do it? Drop the routines and just be badass bikers for a couple of weeks? I already bought the bikes, what do you have to lose?"

And there was something about the black and chrome, the loud purr between John's legs that made John feel a surge of virile power he hadn't felt since his ears came off as a boy. Not that he'd known it then, or would even have been able to name the severance of his ears as the source of his disconnection, but to Josh it was clear. Josh knew the magic the ears possessed, binding him to John the way they did.

On their second day cruising, Josh began to notice a kind of lightness and easy laughter in John's eyes that he had so rarely glimpsed, laughter without meanness in it. Josh's heart fired like a beacon in response, as though finally, after all this time, he'd been able to open something in John to let his beauty seep through. Something like his own love reflected back.

The accident happened just outside of Butte, Montana, when a long-hauler hopped-up on speed tried to overtake them and misjudged the sharpness of the left-leaning curve. Josh's bike skidded out from under him and he shot clear of the tangle, the right side of his body scraping against the asphalt at ninety-five kilometres an hour, fracturing ribs and femur, knocking his helmet so hard the buckle sheared the ear right off.

John Handy's body was a mess of bone, blood, leather, chrome, and muscle, plastered to mush between bike and semi-trailer. They scraped him off the road with shovels and brushes, delicately picking apart flesh from machine before putting him in the burn box.

Josh came to in a corner room of the hospital, looking out on a newly built parkade. He had been transferred back to Vancouver while still in a coma, stable enough to move but the extent of the damage as yet undecided. It had been three weeks already since the accident, John's funeral over and done with, his ashes sitting in an urn on Mrs. Handy's windowsill with the leather pouch encircling it, holding the last remains of her son. She knew what was in the pouch when she found it while cleaning out John's condo. She had given it to him to hold his ears when he had decided to have them severed as a boy, tucked in the medicines her grandmother had shown her as a girl.

Mrs. Handy had spent many wakeful nights petting the soft fur of John's ears as she nursed her baby through the difficult months of infancy. He had been a savage suckler, kicking and scratching at her body, pulling at her hair with his rough hands. She had needed to find such strength to pin him to her long enough to settle him. When the feeding spasms subsided toward sleep she would stroke his silver fur and love him.

John had not been kind to Mrs. Handy. As he grew older he began to find her love for him repulsive. As a man John Handy saw his mother only once every few years. It enraged him to sit in the trailer with her as she sucked on her inhaler between cigarettes, her coughs racking her frail body through the night so she slept one, maybe two hours at a time, waking up to puff, smoke, and sift through pages of the *Reader's Digest* she still had a subscription to after all these years. He'd stay two nights at most and then be on his way, the whole time lavished with remonstrations for not visiting enough and presented with the rich food Mrs. Handy made when he came to town. Food he devoured hungrily, feeling disgusted with himself for his hunger.

Josh told the plastic surgeon he would wait to have his ear done. He knew it was fate when he found the surgeon who had done John's ears as a boy was still practising. It would be tricky, Josh knew, to get a hold of the second ear. He thought about it, but decided the magic would be disrupted if he had just the one silver fox ear attached to the right side of his head. He would have to find a way to be alone with John's remains long enough to take the other ear and leave behind a replica in its place.

Mrs. Handy blamed Josh for John's death. It was Josh, after all, who had bought the bike and enlisted her son to follow him on a ridiculous quest. According to Mrs. Handy, Josh had always been a bad influence on John. Coercing her boy down to the river, getting him into trouble with other boys at school, taking him off to the city and making it so

John was too busy to talk on the phone. Inviting him along on trips to foreign places so that John never came home. Mrs. Handy had always felt Josh was trying to take John away from her, and finally he had.

When Josh called to offer his condolences, the sadness and rage mixed together so she could not tell one from the other.

"Hello?"

"Mrs. Handy? It's Josh, Josh Outage, John's friend. You remember me, from next door?"

She breathed heavily, saying nothing, shaking.

Josh's voice started to tremble, his eyes filling with tears. "I'm so sorry, Mrs. Handy. I loved him too."

She growled, "You dirty little stinking faggot. Fuck'n nerve to call here. Better it had been you!"

She began to hack violently between sobs and desperate gasps, frantically tapping the red icon on her phone so that she missed the mark several times before slamming it into the table, an old hang-up routine from the time when the listener on the other end could still hear the receiver smack down before the line cut out.

She shook in revulsion and despair, rage immobilizing her as she longed to break everything in her home, reduce it all to shards, rip it apart with her teeth. The overwhelm of love and loss, the aching she remembered, thinking of John's body turned to cinders on her mantel, and the way Carl Outage's cock had felt in her mouth all those mornings when John had already caught the bus to school and Vicky over at #13 had pulled her red Sunbird out of the gravel driveway for an early morning shift at Overwaitea. She'd open the curtains just a few inches and turn the lipstick plant flower-side-out so Carl would know on his way home from night shift that she was waiting for him, that Ron Handy was out on opposite shift, having caught the bus an hour and a half earlier, already in his overalls and hard hat for shift change by the time Carl came out of the shower at the dry. She'd wait half an hour, then look out her kitchen window, waiting to see his bedroom curtains open, the wooden dowel he liked to be fucked with standing on end on the windowsill, then she'd walk out the side door, around back, to be let into Carl and Vicky's bright living room through the sliding patio door.

Josh called back and left a message when she did not pick up, voice still shaky, but determined, a wheedling she recognized from the way his father, Carl, had sometimes spoken to her, his voice filled with need, "I have the other ear, Mrs. Handy. I want to bring it to you."

The plan was to find his way into Mrs. Handy's home and somehow switch out the left while handing her the replica of the right.

Josh had scoured thrift stores, but silver fox pelts were hard to find second-hand, and he didn't have a well-to-do granny anywhere nearby who might have one stored away in the attic somewhere from a time when it would have been acceptable, even necessary, when on outings of a certain nature, to have a dead fox draped about the neck. He found a silver fox farm online that was willing to sell him a pair of ears from an imperfect pelt. He'd have to rough them up a bit to make them look older but he was pretty sure he could pass them off.

Although Mrs. Handy watched a lot of crime TV, Josh was pretty sure she didn't have easy access to DNA testing, or insight into his true motives that would lead her to suspect a switch. He hoped his missing right ear would not arouse suspicion, but his hair was long enough to mostly cover the gash, and with a floppy hat, one would have to be really looking to notice.

Josh Outage had a hard time reintegrating into his life once he had John Handy's ears sewn onto the sides of his face. The fur muffled sound and the crisp dead skin made it hard to sleep on his side. He began to hear the world differently. The city made him nervous. He found himself darting through open spaces, always seeking cover, listening for the soft sounds of small creatures rather than the variations in pitch that allow us to discern the meaning of human speech. Josh became unable to decipher the babble around him. He stopped going into the office, just taking contracts that would allow him to work from home. He started ordering all of his groceries online, finding himself less and less able to face the city in daylight. Josh became crepuscular, a lurker in the shadow world.

The instinct to hunt came upon him slowly. He noticed a yearning for the neighbour's cat as she munched wheat grass on the balcony next door. He began stalking her. Unable to focus on writing code when he heard the patio door open.

"What's pretty Penny doing now?" he'd ask her across the grate.

Josh began watching nature videos of foxes on YouTube. He marvelled at how they fed—dainty, yet vicious—red efflorescences splattered across silvery moustaches. Pictures of lost cats started to stack up on neighbourhood telephone poles with increasingly generous rewards. None of the cats came back. During his hunting trips Josh staked out cubbies, cozy dens under porches and brambles where he could spend some time curled up into a warm ball. Although he somehow managed to keep paying the bills, he spent less and less time indoors. His bed had not been slept in for months now, as he had come to prefer the nest of blankets and clothes rumpled underneath his coats hanging in the hall closet, the little toe bones of cats stashed underneath, giving his den an earthy smell.

Another kind of want started inkling in. He could not get Mrs. Handy out of his mind, as though he remembered the taste of her, a sweet warm milk soothing all of his hungers.

Josh set up camp in a copse of pines not far from the trailer park. The still rational part of him thought it was out of kindness, a sense of duty toward Mrs. Handy now that John was gone. But it was mostly hunger that drove him each night to paw through her yard and peer in the backlit windows, her haunting shape cradled in crocheted acrylic afghans in front of the muted old television set John had bought her when he moved out and she talked all the time about feeling lonely. Smoke haze enveloping the eerie flashing silence with a thick sense of the surreal. The long hours of night unwound themselves from clock-time as Josh watched Mrs. Handy and Mrs. Handy sat, slept, smoked, shuffled to the bathroom and back to her couch.

Although Mrs. Handy seemed to exist in a mostly quiet world, the loss of John was turning her already suspicious nature into a virulent tumult — a weary mother with no more mouths to feed. Long, almost sleepless nights in front of the television; by day she took to preparing all of John's favourite meals, only to watch them decay and flourish into mysterious fungal life forms. She herself never touched a bite from the plate, just the requisite tasting as things simmered, to make sure it would come out just the way John liked. Already chain-smoker-thin she began to shrivel. As her body shrank she started to look more and more vulpine. Big socket eyes seeing everything, slight fuzz all over her face, somewhere between red and black.

Mrs. Handy made John on purpose, didn't she though? How else did the fox ears come to be, but for her cunning? Shifter that she was, she had entered a fox den one night and came out full of embryonic kits. In the early days of the pregnancy, shifted back and lost four of them as her womb snapped to its human shape. Bore Ron Handy a son he always suspected had come from elsewhere. Fox ears did not run in his family, and though the wife's kin were shifty folk who might have been the source of such an anomaly, he never saw the more-than-human side of that line either.

After John came into the world, she lost the ability to alter form at will. Motherhood stripped her previous malleability from her—solid and centrifugal force that she became. Whether the early childhood reverence or the later adulthood revulsion her son held for her, her body lost its fluency as her work shifted from self to brood.

When John died, the grief shocked her toward an in-betweenness she had never known. Somewhere between fox and human, unable to fully inhabit either. After John's killer came to return the stolen bits of her son's body, Mrs. Handy knew she was being hunted.

Josh thought he had tricked the old bitch, but after he left, Mrs. Handy pulled the frayed bits of fur from their bag and one sniff told her they were fakes. She could smell the chemical tanning agents all over them, no hint of her boy's scent anywhere.

She knew the ears would find a way back to her, and so she waited. After a few months she began to sense him outside.

Crafty little fuck, she thought, come to finish me off.

The wildness was growing in both of them.

By day he'd return to his burrow, unseeing as she stockpiled her deadliest things, filed her long yellow nails razor-sharp.

He came to her by night. A soft rasping at the door when he thought she was sleeping, he himself unsure of what he intended as he sought the warm breath of her body. All day she had felt him coming, her intentions clear as icicles from the trailer's tin roof holding sunlight on the coldest days of winter. He was surprised at the force of her, the quickness of her frail body launching from the couch, brown rainbow afghan floating to the floor as if in slow motion as her claws dug into the sides of his face and her sharp mouth closed in on his throat. She severed the ears with almost surgical precision, then spat out the taste of him.

Josh Outage was found bleeding and earless two days later on a logging road in the Boundary District, several hours west of the town he'd grown up in. That he'd been attacked by a canid was clear, but the nature of the wounds remained puzzling. He claimed he had fallen on a rock when looking up at a red-tailed hawk during a wilderness jaunt and had been awoken hours later by shearing pain.

He had dragged himself out of the bush bleeding and delirious into the path of a loaded logging truck.

The second time round, the prosthetics were humanoid — hairless, rounded, delicately lobed, and absolutely devoid of magic. Ears that masked him back into the human world, though Josh could not hear out of them — the internal architecture irreparably damaged by Mrs. Handy's yellowed claws. The last sound he ever heard in his life a vulpine shriek unmistakably yelping "Joh-nnn," a haunting soliloquy of mourning.

Her Unspoken Name

She has a human first name but no one except her friend
Di really uses it, and sometimes the checkout ladies at the
grocery store, though most of them call her Mrs. Handy. It's
just the older ones who remember her from before, whose
kids grew up with her son, John. Who used to see her in
there with him when he was just a little boy with fox ears,
strapped into the spot up front, and then later as a sulky
teenager with human ears and pimples all over his face
who wouldn't make eye contact with them, just mumbled
replies from under his hood when they asked about his day.
Those ones call her Lucia because some of them grew up
with her, and knew her from before she was Mrs. Handy.
She used to be called ma, before John died. She thought of
herself as ma when John was around. Di calls her Lucia.
Lucia Maria when she's feeling playful.

Lucia thinks of herself by her fox name. It's not the kind of name that can be made with human mouth parts, so even if she wanted to, she wouldn't be able to tell her human folk the name she knows herself by. Even her son, John, didn't know it, or at least she's pretty sure he didn't, and if her mom did, she never let on. Her grandmère Jonquille knew it. She's the one that spoke it to her, yipped it to her as she sang her to sleep when Lucia was a young girl and grandmère was still alive.

"Lucia" is good enough. It has something of her movements in it. A story attached that moves through human time, time which is filled almost constantly with smoke, not that she notices she's smoking. Only notices when she's not.

Lucia appreciates the honesty of cows. It's why she's never bitten one. Never mind their size could wreck her, and chances are nil she'd ever get a meal out of one unless it was so close to death it was already on the ground. Sure, she could pay for its flesh at the grocery, where someone else had done the killing for her but Lucia, unlike some of her fox kin, does not like to eat the long dead. When she feasts she wants the blood to rush into her, feel the life flow in. Still, she goes to the grocery to buy the foods she needs to cook the meals John would have liked, plus some things for herself—milk and coffee, tea biscuits and Lucky Charms, things to put in her cupboards so she isn't just putting in cartons of cigarettes. The biscuits and sugary marshmallows keep her tongue company, because she has to eat sometimes and she doesn't have the will to hunt lately.

Lucia doesn't leave the house much now. Groceries once a week, Di's on Sundays. She feels so much older, like the last eight months since John died have been a decade of her life. A decade on replay, in which she ages dramatically, but time feels stuck somehow. It feels so hard to get around now that John is missing from the world, hard to feel purpose. TV distracts her. She talks to Di about it. They like to watch the same programs. They still watch *Days of Our Lives* after all these years, though they have trouble connecting with the new storylines, the kids of the characters whose intrigues used to fill their days with gossip back when their kids were the same age as the characters' kids on the show. Now that John is dead it hurts Lucia to watch those soap kids as adults fucking up their lives. She hates them for reliving their parents' TV mistakes, hates them too because so often their loved ones come back from the dead and she knows her little boy won't.

Lucia inherited some power, but she doesn't totally know what to do with it. That's why John was born with fox ears that got stuck that way, unable to shift between fox and human form. She knew as soon as she saw her baby that she had fucked the magic up somehow, that he would never learn how to use it himself. She pretended for a long time that things might change, watching him with his little friend from next door, watching how his little friend looked at the ears, and at her boy, trying to mask her disappointment in John with overindulgent love, doting on every small success that marked him as better than the other boys. She hoped otherwise, but knew for certain by the time he started school that he was just a boy with fox ears who wished nothing more than to be a boy with regular fleshy pink lobes like the other boys in his class. Still, she refused to even talk about it with him when he'd ask to have them removed. It took years of fits and tantrums, begging and screaming matches, until she acquiesced to the surgery. She knew if she didn't, he would hate her the rest of his life. Hate her through the strangeness of his own body.

If she had known better magic, if the old ones hadn't been taken from her, maybe she could have found a way to use the ears to bring him back now that he was gone. Not in his human form, but in fox form, the way he never really was. She gave herself a year to try, but she didn't have the right knowledge, and she didn't have others to help her know it.

She doesn't know why he got stuck between, only that it was painful for him. Or she thinks it was. That's the tricky thing with magic. You think you know how to do things the way your grandmère and her grandmère did them, but maybe you've been living in a world that changes the way magic works and you forget to offer the right medicines before you tap on the sprit folks' shoulders? Or maybe it's just that the spirit folks want to play a trick on you because spirit folks are tricky. And really, why shouldn't magic change the way it works from incantation to incantation?

Everything Lucia's watched and read about magic makes it seem like once you learn the spells and get the medicines right, once you figure out how to dwell unflinchingly in your own power, then you become masterful, know how to be fully who and what you are. But she doesn't believe that's how it works. She thinks there's always a little bit of unknown, or a lot.

It's not like Sparrowhawk and Harry, and all those other heroes and heroines from fantasy novels whose names she can't remember now because they were always following the same quest, fucking up a bunch until finally. Finally, they came into their full being and figured it out. Most of them anyway, though later, Ursula Le Guin did go back and rewrite Sparrowhawk, make him lose his magic and just live life out as a regular man because he used up too much and now, Ursula decided, it was time for girl dragon people to embody the unwieldy power of dragons and girls, not just be relegated to the forest and caves as witches who could never learn the most potent magics, the magics ensconced in institutions guarded by old white-bearded men.

These aren't her grandmère's stories, but they're the ones John loved to hear her read to him. The ones he'd sit still for while she stroked his ears. John was old enough then to pretend he was too old to read those books, though he did take them when she offered—he didn't even have the ears anymore, but it was the same story, pretty much, more sophisticated marketing, but the same magic. They were letting girls do it in this version, but the girls still didn't get to be the strongest wizards, just got to kiss or make babies with the boys who were.

Lucia didn't know her grandmère's and her nonno's stories anyways. She was too young when grandmère Jonquille died. And her mother, who went by Marie, had taken full force to the Catholicism they made her learn in school, hanging saints all over the house for different purposes that Lucia couldn't keep straight, going on all the time about angels whenever things got confusing or hurt too much, or seemed too good to be true. Angels could do miracles just because they felt like it, not just swoop down to clean up messes after the worst things took place. Marie told Lucia John's ears were all part of God's plan, said nothing to her about what grandmère Jonquille had been, because Marie thought it was devilish. Marie feared for them, feared Lucia's magic might have to do with demons somehow, and that maybe with enough praying it could all be okay. So Marie prayed for them. For John and Lucia, for Jonquille, but not for herself, because it was selfish to ask God for things that were just for you.

The creature that became Lucia was born into darkness, blind and deaf, it took her weeks of suckling next to her brothers and sisters, before she knew light for the first time. The first time she shifted she was six months old, ready to breed for the first time. It was strange for her to find herself in fetal form again, light muted through thick pink walls, nearly total darkness. The sound of her mother's voice reverberating through the amniotic liquid filling her ears, as if in agony. She came into her human body at the same moment baby Lucia started her descent into the birth canal, confused by the drive in her to find breath and light.

When she came out she cried with a voice unfamiliar in her mouth, calmed only by the latch she knew instinctively to find with her awkward pink lips. Called forth by grand-mère Jonquille to a mother as intimate to her as forever, even though she'd never known her until then.

Lucia's mother, Marie, had not been a shifter. Because of the times it was too dangerous a gift for young Jonquille to gift to the baby whose name got changed to Marie. Even though Jonquille tried to hide her, spent years moving west with her husband and the baby, she was eventually forced to send her to school. Where they named her daughter Marie Morgan and taught her to feel shame.

Though as a very young girl, the girl who became Marie had often wished for her mother's fluidity of form, something she saw only in the rarest of times when Jonquille was feeling vulnerable enough to show herself fully; by the time she became a woman, Marie had disregarded this longing as a garbled memory from childhood. A memory of her mother from before she had been taken from her, mixed up with misremembered stories that no longer belonged to who she had become, to the world she had learned to live in.

As a newlywed Marie moved even farther west with her husband, Antonio Pelucci, who had recently come over from the old country and was on his way to meet his brother to work in the underground mines. She became pregnant shortly after arriving, and shortly after that, she received word that her father had died. It was decided that Jonquille would come to help care for the baby. Marie did not know that Jonquille would or could change her perfect girl into the creature Lucia became when the hormones of adolescence kicked the shifting into high gear. She had assumed these things were no longer possible, that the old magics were no longer around, that the angels from heaven had convinced them, with their heavenliness, to stay out of human affairs.

Jonquille died when Lucia was still too young to know what she was, so she had no one to guide her through those first shifting years of adolescence. Her sexuality magnified by fox hormones coursing alongside human ones in ways neuroscientists could not even begin to explain the workings of. Life went to total schism for a while. She left her mother and her mother's Church and went for a while to the town downriver, which was far enough that Marie didn't know where she was, just stayed at home praying for her baby girl to come back from wherever the devil had taken her.

Lucia met Ron Handy when she was seventeen, and for a while he calmed her, made her feel like she had somewhere solid to come back to. When she was with Ron she felt like she could stay in human form, went almost three months without shifting. When he got a job at the mine after high school they moved back to Lucia's hometown, into one of the trailer parks that had just gone up along the highway. As soon as Lucia found herself home alone, playing house while Ron was out on twelve-hour night shifts, the wildness started to creep back in. No longer held in sway by promises of a possible future in which she would be different from what she was, Lucia began to find that she had patterns to being human. She learned how to do "shift work" too, finding herself yearning for fox form as Ron's days off ended and she packed his lunch box with bologna sandwiches and home-baked cookies.

They had a few good years, her and Ron, doing shift work together. Though Ron didn't know about Lucia's work world. So long as she seemed to be what he thought she was, Ron was happy to have things as they were. With Ron gone for fourteen hours a day or night, Lucia had plenty of time to play with her inherited magics. Instead of being scared of what she was, thinking herself sinful because of her mother's fears, she started to remember stories grand-mère had told her. Stories from when she was a little girl and grandmère Jonquille was braiding her hair, stories that did not seem to her so different from the ones mama told from the Bible, or the other ones she read in picture books, different ideas coming together in her mind for how to place herself in the world. Stories in which people and creatures were always doing impossible things—creatures wearing people clothes and living in people houses, people walking on water or turning to salt or falling out of gardens, mama rabbits in big galoshes fishing for baby rabbits with carrots, hugging them to make them come home.

The stories were all mixed up so Lucia didn't know how to understand what was real and what wasn't, though she was starting to feel she might be able to choose, instead of always being scared she was getting it wrong. The way mama was always scared of getting it wrong because so many of mama's stories were about how other stories were bad and the people who believed them were bad. This never made sense to Lucia. She knew grandmère wasn't bad and could tell mama was scared so much of the time, and it seemed to Lucia like the stories were made to make her feel that way.

Lucia remembered grandmère Jonquille talking about when the ancestors didn't have to stay in the same bodies all the time and how sometimes they were in the stars or in the clouds and all the creatures were kinfolk with different stories to tell. That sometimes there were girls who went away to be beavers and their families missed them but understood. That beavers were important to the world, needing to do beaver work for all the other kinds of people to have ponds and waterways to travel. Lucia knew she had fox work to do, but didn't know what it was. So she foxed in the forest when Ron was at the mine. She dug a den under the back shed that Ron buried whenever he caught sight of it. She went up the mountain, never as far as she wanted to go because she always had to be back to fix things up for Ron coming home. And Ron never saw any of it, or if he did, he didn't say anything for her to know he had.

It was a dream that made Lucia seek a fox mate. A dream that was with her whenever she slept. She kept dreaming of her babies. When she was in human form the babies were foxes, she petted their soft heads, cooed into their ears. When she slept as a fox, her babies were human babies, she licked their pink skin clean. She never ever dreamt of the in-between baby that John became—John, who she put everything into. Weird corruption that he was. John fixed her and wrecked her a little at the same time. Keeping her home, keeping her human. She loved him and felt horrified by him. Did everything to mask that horror.

Vicky and Carl Outage moved into the trailer next door when Lucia and Vicky were both pregnant, a few months after Lucia had become Mrs. Handy.

"It was beautiful, Lucy, the whole process. Like the pain had a sweetness to it. It almost felt like I was floating," Vicky said to Lucia when Lucia stopped by with a pot of stew a week after Josh was born. Lucia Handy held the stew at an awkward angle, struggling not to spill it with John, barely a month old, flailing in a sling strapped to her chest. "I had no idea how empowering it would be. I'm sorry I didn't ask, I just hadn't realized until I went through it myself," Vicky added, her eyes never leaving Josh's face. "What was it like for you, Lucy?"

"Uh, I don't know Vicky, hard."

Lucia felt disgust for the Outage boy from the first time she saw him. His perfect round face, Vicky and her painless birth, and it hadn't waned a few months later when Vicky told her he was sleeping through the night at four months old.

As the boys grew older, Lucia felt unease at the way Vicky's boy played with her boy. He seemed to love John so easily, while her love for him was bound up in the intensity of magics she did not understand, always taking hold of her in strong aberrant ways. Josh was always watching John, mimicking him, seeing John in ways she could not see him.

Josh was foreign to her as fuck, with the sorts of saccharine kindness Vicky was always lavishing on Carl in public, and on her, who always seemed to be needing help of one kind or the other. She was so much alone. Since Ron had stopped giving anything to her and the boy but the weekly grocery budget, after seeing the way John came out. He lived alongside them as though they didn't exist. The sort of generosity Josh and his mother showed her and John always made her feel lacking somehow, like her loneliness was branded on her, a deep burning shame.

Looking back she thinks the hate wasn't so much bitterness as foresight. She thinks maybe she could see it in him from the start. Not a genuine love but something more covetous — drawn to the magic without understanding where it came from. Always wanting what her son had, drawing John into a world made for boys like Josh, boys who thought the world belonged to them, that they were deserving of everything it had to offer.

If she had followed her instinct, found a way to get Josh out of their lives early on, John might still be with her. If she had told Vicky straight up about Carl. How he had fucked her on their bed, their kitchen floor — so clean it was like watching a commercial — Mrs. Handy looking under the fridge and stove, hoping to find evidence of the dust and debris that lined every crevice of her home, finding nothing. How Carl liked to lick her as she sat on Vicky's washing machine, gripping Vicky's perfect peach towels in her hands. How he had grovelled and she threatened to burn his house down if he didn't leave, harm anything she could, give explicit details to his wife and son about the things they had done together in their family home, the things he had confessed to doing with Becky Henlie and Marcy Faraccone in the same places, when he thought she was in love with him and he wanted to show her how little respect he had for his perfect wife.

Mrs. Handy scared Carl Outage away when the things that had once excited her turned into things she found herself loathing him for. When his tongue started feeling like a dog's—too wet and hot behind her ears, his spit cold and sticky on her cunt. She had a husband already; she didn't need another. If Mrs. Handy had told Vicky, she might have left too, taken the boy her son loved away with her.

Lucia wondered how Vicky couldn't see it, the way Carl undressed every one of his boy's friends' mothers with his eyes. She had loved the way it felt to finally take her clothes off for him, watch his hardness turn to throbbing, an urgent need to have her, feeling a bit superior, for once, to perfect perky Vicky. Fucking Carl had never been about Carl. It had been about being wanted—to prove to herself she could be better than Vicky, that her body was something to be lusted after.

Her own husband had touched her only once since John was born, and it had given her no pleasure. He was not mean, but his disinterest was also a certain kind of cruelty. He barely acknowledged John, spent all his time off work in his shop, out hunting, or down at the Legion, so that by the time John was five years old, he had stopped even trying to talk to his father. Ron bought the next trailer over and moved into it when John was seven.

Vicky Outage had been Vicky Similovich. Lucia had known her since Vicky's family moved to town in grade five. Vicky's father had been brought in when the new mine had started up, he had been out East before then, working for the Company in a mine that was now shut down.

Vicky's daddy was the Big Boss Man. That's what Lucia heard her dad say: "Big Boss Man."

Somehow it seemed dirty when she heard him say it. So none of the other girls liked Vicky. Because her dad was the Big Boss Man, but they all wanted to be her friend so she would invite them over to her brand new house on the acreage outside of the new townsite where they kept white horses and chickens with puffy feathers on the tops of their heads, where they had something called French doors and a liquor cabinet with amber- and gold-coloured liquids that in grade seven Vicky would show Lucia how to take sips out of and fill the bottles back up with water, just enough that it didn't taste watered down.

"Here, Lucy, come in here, quick before mommy comes back inside."

"Are you sure we should be in here, Vicky?"

"It's okay, mommy and daddy won't know, I do it all the time. Taste this one, my daddy says it's a hundred dollars just for this bottle, he brought it from Calgary last time he went for work. It's probably worth more money than your parents' car."

"It smells bad, like burnt bacon."

"It gets you drunk fast."

"I don't want to get drunk. Mama says it's sinful to get drunk. You're not supposed to steal from your parents!"

"Lucy, it's not sinful as long as you just do it for fun! Here I'll go first."

Vicky took two big gulps then handed the bottle over, pinching Lucia until Lucia finally took a drink. Lucia felt those liquids burning going down; they weren't like the sweet red wine her dad brewed, that she was allowed a small watered-down glass of for Christmas dinner. She felt like Vicky had burned her. Coughed and spat some out her nose.

"You're such a baby, Lucy!" Vicky said with bright flashy eyes. "Quick, give me another swig. Now we have to put just as much water back as we drank so daddy won't know."

Lucia went over to Vicky's maybe three times, but she didn't like the stupid games Vicky wanted to play with her paper dolls, always complaining they didn't like living in a stupid small town. Vicky's dolls getting all the nice clothes while the ones she let Lucia play with had to wear ripped pieces and aprons Vicky drew stains on with her coloured markers. Lucia thought Vicky was mean and couldn't hide the fact that she didn't like her, the way the other girls did, pretending to be friends then saying things about her behind her back.

Lucia didn't like Vicky's house either. All the rooms with things you weren't allowed to touch in them. She felt confused by the lines of dolls in pink dresses on the wainscotting in Vicky's bedroom. Vicky had told her that mama had let her choose the faded yellow colour that Lucia thought looked like horse pee for the paint on what Lucia heard as "Wayne's cutting." She thought maybe Vicky's dad was named Wayne and he had cut the boards halfway up the wall and made a shelf for the dolls. But she knew Vicky's dad's name was Sasha, which she thought was a girl's name. But she didn't want to ask Vicky who Wayne was and why there were dolls you weren't allowed to play with everywhere that had glassy eyes always staring off into space.

Lucia thought of those dolls every time she was lying naked on Vicky's floor with Vicky's husband's cock working its way inside her, wondering if he could make Vicky cum the way he made her cum, when he turned her over on her knees and fucked her from behind, tickling her clit with his fingers. Wondering after, his limp dick dripping, how Vicky had ended up in a trailer just like her, about why her daddy hadn't bought Vicky and Carl a nice house in town or built one for her on all the land he owned. About how Vicky had become a sickly sweet woman with a fuckhead for a husband and a perfect loving son, when she had been a snobby thieving little rich girl who thought she was worth so much more than every other girl in town.

Vicky moved out of her trailer into a townhouse on Hemlock a few years after Carl left, when John and Josh had just started high school. And when Josh left after high school, Vicky left too. Lucia doesn't know where she went, just gone, to the city maybe, she thinks she heard something about Vicky going to the city. Vicky's dad's place was bought by one of the local boys during the '90s bust when the mine shut down for a few years and a bunch of folks left town. Vicky's dad among them. No more Big Boss Man. The Company that owned the mine now was some multinational—Big Boss Men didn't live in town anymore, just flew as close as they could get, then drove in with unmarked white suvs when things happened they couldn't deal with remotely or through the little boss men they hired on salary to hand down policies to the union boys they now called "team members."

Ron Handy still lived next door to Mrs. Handy, paid the pad rent for both the trailers, filed his and Mrs. Handy's taxes, made sure both woodsheds were full come winter, and that the walkways and driveways were plowed. He would drop packages of cuts into Mrs. Handy's outdoor freezer from the animals he shot and butchered. After all, they were still married. Mrs. Handy, in exchange, put yogurt containers of stews and aluminum trays of lasagnas and meat pies and buns to go with them in the freezer in Mr. Handy's shed. Once a week, on Fridays, when Ron was out for lunch at the mall with Doug Henlie, where they stayed all afternoon to play chess, sipping on the free refills, Mrs. Handy went over and stripped his bed, laundered the sheets, cleaned up the small bits of grey and black hair all around the bathroom sink, changed the blades on his razor, scrubbed the toilet and bathtub, vacuumed the rugs she had brought over to cover the bare plywood floors where Ron had pulled up the old shag and never replaced it with anything, and washed the yellow linoleum floors in the kitchen and bathroom. Now that Mr. Handy was retired, it was easy, his lunch out always falling on the same day. When he was still working, Mrs. Handy had had to keep track of his shifts, remembering which day his second day off was, arranging her plans around that.

Despite the care Mr. and Mrs. Handy exchanged with one another, they had not spoken since Mr. Handy moved next door and the original agreement was made. They left notes on Mr. Handy's table on cleaning day if they needed to communicate anything to one another. When Ron retired, he let Mrs. Handy know that she could come on Fridays from now on. It suited her to wipe Mr. Handy's hair from the sink once a week instead of once every couple of days, as she did when he still lived with them. To smell him on the sheets for a few brief moments before laundering them, instead of it wafting up from under the covers every time he turned over in the night. And it suited Ron not to have to live among them, to do his duty, as he had promised, but not have to live with John's whining and screaming, his sulkiness, the daily complaints that Ron was not living in the house the way Lucia wanted it lived in.

When John moved away for university, the arrangement remained the same. Ron left a thousand-dollar cheque on the table in an envelope that said *John* on it after his graduation, his closure of fatherly duty. He continued to hand over half of what he earned to Mrs. Handy, part of which she always squirrelled away for John, until John graduated and got a job with that company he was always travelling around for. John made more money in a month than Mrs. Handy did in four, especially after Mr. Handy went on pension.

Mrs. Handy's feelings from Mr. Handy were muted. She had once felt despair, rage, and a deep penetrating sadness to think of his abandoning John, shutting him out of the barest forms of intimacy. There was a time, when John was still an infant, and then learning to speak, when she used to call Ron "papa," talk about what he was doing as though he were part of their family, thinking maybe if she did, he would feel something for his son. She knew he thought John wasn't his, the way he looked at her when John was born—those beautiful ears, still wetted to his head—the disgust he felt for both of them that changed the warmth he'd once given her into a slow quiet resentment measured out over time into complete disregard.

When John died, Lucia wrote on the notepad, *He's gone.* They exchanged nothing else. Kept on as they had always done. The one small thing Mr. Handy noticed, but said nothing about, was the change in food showing up in his freezer. Over the years Lucia had been so consistent, cooking him the kinds of heavily salted foods he loved—deer stews with potatoes, salt, and carrot, thickened with white flour; lasagnas with ground elk, mozzarella, and tomato sauce made only with canned tomatoes, sugar, and salt;

fried pork chops and potatoes in cream sauce; white rice and corned beef casserole the years when he didn't get any wild game for her to cook with. Now though, there were things like masalas and Thai green curries showing up, things with chickpeas and an herb called sumac—pungent things his tongue did not know how to make sense of so that he ate only bites before having to stop, overwhelmed by the savoury-sweet smells. Ron lost weight during Lucia's mourning; his body still inextricably tied to the feelings Lucia felt for John.

There had been a month after John died in which the meals had been slight variations of the ones Ron liked— real close, but a bit more lavish somehow, with little differences Ron could taste but did not quite understand. He didn't know Lucia was waiting, paying homage to the one thing her boy and husband had shared—an appetite for her rich homey foods—John's portions turning to fungal forests on her kitchen table, Ron's safely stashed away in his deep freeze.

Then things changed. Ron knew nothing about what was going on in the trailer next door. He had no idea that Lucia was going to try her hand at necromancy now that she finally had both of John's ears back, that she planned to spend a year seeing if she could find a way to draw his spirit fully forth into the pieces she had left of him—for them both to slip into their fox bodies and return to the more-than-human world.

John's ashes sat in a cedar urn on the mantel, encircled by the medicine pouch Lucia had given him as a boy when he had first had his fox ears removed — the ears held close in the sweetness of dried sage and cedar sprigs, quietly doing their healing work, bundles tied and tucked into the urn. Lucia wanted the ears held in safe magics while she searched the forest at night in fox form for ancient voices that might speak to her, whisper answers for the longing in her heart. Answers she knew might be dangerous.

To keep herself busy during the day, outside of the fox-seeking hours of darkness, Lucia decided to learn how to cook foods from the places John had travelled. To pay homage to the way he had walked in the world, even if she didn't understand how or what he'd been doing when doing it. Di brought her books from the library on Indian and Thai cooking, found one called *A Taste of Morocco*. She ate so little herself, most of it went into Mr. Handy's freezer. John's portions she now burned in the fire, sending them into the spirit world. She tasted bits of the food, licking at it with her fox tongue, tearing into the raw spiced meats with her canines before throwing the other bits into hot oil, smelling deeply as they sizzled.

A month after the first anniversary of John's death Mr. Handy was surprised to find Di knocking at his door. His freezer was full to the brim with meals he had no interest in eating, and because it was summer and there was no fire next door, he hadn't noticed that Mrs. Handy had not been around for a while. Di was looking a bit frantic, asking if he'd seen Lucia, if he could bring his key over to open up her place, since she was afraid to go in alone.

At first everything seemed to be as it always was — TV on, stale smoke smell wafting out at them when they opened the door. Mr. Handy hadn't been in the house since the last time the fridge had been replaced — ten years ago, maybe, so he didn't notice anything out of place. But Di saw right away when she went into the living room that the urn and pouch were gone, and she knew Lucia was not coming back.

A few months after Lucia's disappearance Ron Handy received a strange letter for his wife from that boy who had lived next door, Carl Outage's boy. By this time Di had taken anything she had thought worth keeping from her friend's home so that Ron could sell the trailer. He missed the food, at least the food he had grown accustomed to in all the years but the last. But with the money he got from selling Lucia's trailer, no longer having to pay two pad rents, and no longer having to split his pension, he had enough to go out to eat more often, and Di, god knows why, dropped off a casserole for him every couple of weeks that helped get him through. Lucia no longer had her own postal box now that she was presumed dead, so Ron ended up with her mail in his. He read through the *Reader's Digest* until the subscription ran out, tossed the junk mail—all the prize packages for sweepstakes that Lucia must have filled out in her spare time, there being so goddamn many of them. He had cancelled the credit card, closed her bank account, and sold the car so there were no more renewal notices or bank statements coming. The envelope read Mrs. Lucia Handy in a beautiful left-tilted calligraphy, beautiful enough that Ron noticed it was beautiful.

Dear Mrs. Handy,

It is my sincerest hope that you will read this letter. No doubt you will be tempted to burn it, or rip it to shreds, judging by what you did to my face when you took John's ears from me. I want you to know first that I know who you are, that I heard you speak your name when we were circling one another, that I would have called it back to you, had you given me time. I cannot spell it with these letters to prove it to you, it would only come out malformed, a rendition. And now that the ears are gone, I couldn't speak it back to you, even if I wanted to.

I also need you to understand something about John, something you never understood—what I was to him, how my love kept him grounded. I have clarity now that I didn't before. All those years, like I was being haunted by something, driven to stay near him,

and after he died, I couldn't stop thinking about his
ears. It was an instinct, to take them from you and
have him become part of me.

    If only you would have listened to me when I
came to you, instead of doing what you did, would you
have seen how I had become part of John, or him part
of me? Maybe not, maybe you could never really see
him. You saw only the way things didn't work out the
way you wanted them to.

    Maybe I couldn't really see him either though; in
the end he slipped away from me too.

    You brought him into the world and took him back
out. We both loved him, needed him, and what are
we left with? Something went out of the ears when
you took them from me. I can't feel him anymore, so
I can only assume that John is free, or that you did
something to free him. And I'm glad for that. Maybe
he can get some peace now from always thinking
he should be something he wasn't, like what he was
wasn't right somehow. I know you did what you could
to make him beautiful, and maybe it wasn't the kind of
beauty you wanted, but it was beautiful anyway.

With respect and forgiveness,

Joshua Carl Outage

Part Four

Homing

The Teeny Ghost People
and Their Garments

Part 1: Little Fear Stories

There is almost a little bit of fear, it licks the borders of elation.

Tina has a regular-sized head, what she thinks of as a run-of-the-mill post-baby body, hazel eyes with so much soul in them that if you actually manage to see through the tense outer layers of her face, you might get stuck there for a while. Her hair though, it's extraordinary, so most people end up there when she leaves it unbound, which is rarely.

She sits on the bus eating corn nuts. They're salty and crunchy and delicious. She likes the corniness of them.

The fear has a dull hotness to it, you would probably call it warm.

Tina is going between places. Like most of the people on the bus. She gets on at one place and gets off at another, then walks a bit. Then she goes to the place she is going, stays there doing things, walks back out, onto the bus again in the other direction, and walks back home. It is a regular day in the movement world, but not a regular day in Tina's psyche—because of the warm fear and how it takes her out of the movements she is going through. Puts her in a world out there.

Tina's children overwhelm her, even though she loves them. She wonders if everyone is overwhelmed by their children, or just mothers, or mothers and fathers, just in different ways. It seems easier for fathers to turn it off somehow, not be consumed by them. Whatever else Tina is doing, there is always a small bit of guilt gnawing at her that she is doing it away from the children, that by not being there and giving them all of herself, she is perhaps harming them a little. Or not doing her absolute best by them. Her absolute best which cannot soothe the world for them. Because she is not enough for them in the world. How could she be? Her body made them and then suckled them to life for some years so she is tricked into the feeling that without her tender vigilance their being will suffer. She has been duly warned that she must bond them properly to her so they will not become monstrous. They are a bit monstrous anyway. Just like she is a bit monstrous among them. Probably they'll turn out to be fine humans and hopefully they will not disregard her or be emotionally compromised by what she did not give, or what she gave too much of. Hopefully she will remember to be interested in them for who they become and continue to be curious about them in the world as beings separate from but connected to herself, unlike the way Tina's own mother sees her—as an extension of herself always needing motherly analysis on the right way to be in the world.

Other people are interested in Tina for the first time in a long while. They are interested in things Tina has created, not just the way her ass curves or the statements she is making with her wardrobe, not just her baked goods and community fundraising contributions. Tina took the teeniest garments, made for the teeniest ghosts that she had been crafting worlds out of in her secret time, and introduced them into the public sphere. These teeny ghost garments, and the non-visible but somehow perceivable bodies that inhabit them, have taken on a life of their own, and other people have perceived some semblance of the magic.

Something Tina has put into the world is of interest to people. Something that is just hers. Though it's not really. Or at least Tina doesn't see it that way. A little bit Tina found the ghosts who wanted garments and a little bit she made them up by making garments for them. Tina played with bits of cloth she found around the house when she was going through the children's drawers, sorting through things that had gotten too small or stained or tattered.

Clothing with memories worn deeply into the rips, snags, stains, and tears. Memories she did not want to throw into the trash. Tina was playing with things that her children would no longer wear, imagining versions of them without the parts that drove Tina crazy — just privately feeling the full force of the joyous, marvellous, heartwarming things that made her feel right as a mother. The teeny ghost people wanted to be her children too. To light her up this way, to feel warmed by her affections.

The teeniest ghost beings came and she clothed them. She made up entire wardrobes according to the tastes they developed as they moved their bodies around in cloth. The ghost beings invited Tina to see them, and Tina was still enough to see. She got compelled to give them coziness. After the first time she glimpsed the teeny ghost people playing around in the children's clothes she could tell the ghost beings were cold. They seemed to always be shivering around her when she sat still enough to sense them. At first it was just to shelter them out of their coldness, to warm them into an overwhelming domestic world in curious little ways. To take what she was given and play with it intently.

Once the ghost beings got cozy they wanted to get out on the town. They wanted to show off their digs, and they thought Tina should let them. So Tina found a site that talked about how to get your work seen and created an online platform that a lot of people thought was worth clicking on, and in this way she brought the ghost people between worlds. It doesn't matter that much to Tina, or to the ghost beings, that folks see only the garments and not the beings in them. They talk about the indication of presence and use words like "ephemera of domesticity" to describe what they see. They talk about "potent post-consumer maternalism" and the ghost beings giggle and jiggle their butts around to make Tina laugh.

Tina laughs at the quirkiness of their antics, but sometimes she is still afflicted by a hot fear. It tenses the body to pounding and sweaty palms. Sometimes there is cold fear, which tenses the body differently. Hot fear rages. It builds out and wants to clack against things loudly. Cold fear shrinks the body in, a worminess wanting to crawl itself inside. Warm fear is not so raucous. Warm fear can be a little bit glittery, a little bit compelling. A little bit warm. Comfy fear. That's the kind of fear Tina works for. Tina's little girl would call it trickle-rainbow-unicorn fear. It's like when you get mad and scared and you're not sure which comes first and you have to fight about it, then you start to feel less mad but you're still a bit scared and your face wants to love again but your body isn't ready yet. Trickle-rainbow-unicorn fear is when you want to resolve yourself back in to love but still feel shaky about it, all tossed up and vulnerable, but there's a bit of light in it so the colours get all hoppy and refract off your sad madness and you think of unicorns to help you remember magic. Magic helps. It makes you feel real but not crazy.

Tina thinks it's funny to use words like "potency" and "maternalism" together, to give presence in the public sphere to the "ephemera of domesticity" created by potent mothering. Because mothers are mostly uninteresting to people, unless they are being judged or venerated. There's just not a lot of interest in the in-between, which is really where all the living happens.

Fathers look like shelves, or statues, like car-part manuals and boardrooms. They look like men in white coats who are experts on women's reproduction but can't bring their wives to vaginal orgasm. It takes too much time to create the intimacy needed for a slow build and epic internal reverberation, for the wholeness or holiness of that. If they see themselves as kind men, they'll lavish some post-cum fondling on the clitoris to call forth an external release that doesn't require deep bonding. Then they can feel that everyone's been satisfied. They know a lot about nerve endings and pleasure sensation and their fingers are tender because their hands are always gloved in latex. Not like the rough calloused fingers of farmers, some of whom can still find gentleness, because they know how to touch seedlings without harming them.

Tina's hair is big. Very big. Thick and coarse, like horse hair, but with some softness to it. It is also kinky. The kind of curl that doesn't undulate but whacks about in fits and starts, sometimes looping lazily then tightening itself all up and round and over and back on every strand of her head.

It's a private thing, this epic blooming. She keeps it tightly braided. Most people don't even know about it. Sometimes even Tina forgets. She hasn't decided yet if when she goes naked to the grave she'll ask to have it bound or let herself rest and rot amid its opulence. She *has* specified that she wishes to go naked to the grave.

Tina's fear and Tina's teeniest ghost worlds take form in her living room, emerging as quirky vignettes in which the teeny ghost people shine like the brightest stars in a world that otherwise doesn't see them. During the daytime, Tina's making space is littered with children's toys and art supplies, cooking utensils pilfered from the kitchen, bits of cut-up yarn. After bedtime, she sweeps the evidence of all her children's vibrant living into piles that seem to have some order to them. As the night unravels, the room returns to disarray — Tina sitting with her own supplies splayed around her, sipping wine, listening to the radio, her hair spiralling around her face.

Tina is absorbed in creative reverie, barely listening to the murmur, and is all of a sudden confounded by the intrusion of an astronaut's radio certainty that space desires colonization. His hopefulness that we could do it better than we have before. The woman talk show guest tries to explain to him about carefulness. About listening carefully to stones instead of calling them resources. He knows he is a good man and this goodness makes his approach to discovery wondrously banal. He thinks curiosity is apolitical. That good intentions are good enough. That we should all work to fund white men's dreams. The woman says maybe instead we could direct these energies to healing that which has already been damaged so heartily by white men's dreams. She says in different words that they do not want to fix what their dreams have damaged, instead just direct their desires elsewhere, so they can continue to drive for the same dreams. Dream them in outer space instead of attending to the ongoing damage those desires do to the sentient world's dreaming. To the dreams of marginalized dreamers.

Meanwhile, Tina thinks, marginalized dreamers continue to dream. Maybe they are dreaming of a world where everyone shares candy, even the ones with the biggest guns? Or maybe they are dreaming of a world so kind it's unbearable, so kind that we start to sing songs about rupture and then heal these ruptures with song?

Tina's smart phone doesn't have an app for that, and even if it did she would have a cold fear of using it, worried about what she might become if her fingers were tending all the time to those smooth buttons, the sensate glass screen.

On the bus Tina thinks about the things she will bring with her to the showing. Things to ground her fear, so it will not pollute her when she goes to the place that people have asked her to come to in order that they can honour her makings. A place that has a sense of glitter about it. She does not want to be effaced by the glitter. Get caught up in a kind of magic that doesn't belong to her. Tina wants to know her power well enough to walk amongst other people's magic and stay grounded in her own. She has spent many years learning the contours of other people's magic, trying to learn what feeds into her own. Her work will be to gather the things she needs for the grounding. Her psyche helps her plan a future bus trip to gather what she needs. Maybe the children will help her. They like to learn about ceremony, even though it's difficult to be in ceremony when she is showing them the manners of thankfulness. The manners of asking. The manners of recognition, despite the uncertainty. Tina and the children will bring the teeny ghost beings along in the over-the-top outdoor collection they had Tina design. Ridiculous getups that the teeny ghost people act so outdoor enthusiast in, looking like they are prepared to go on a week-long safari in a remote African wilderness: minuscule Tilley hats and khaki cargo pants with seven pockets apiece that Tina cursed over when trying to stitch in workable buttons so their tiny field instruments would not fall out. When really they are just taking a bus ride to the edges of suburbia. The ghost beings are so weighted down by their gear they can barely trek the length of the driveway so Tina's youngest girl has to pack them in her Tonka Jeep, making it seem like she's just a little girl bringing her toy along on the bus. It's a lot of extra baggage, but they need the ghost beings to help them properly identify what they need. Because they are so finicky about fashion and love to get out and about, the

ghost beings may trade their ancestral memories of ceremony for weather-appropriate outerwear and a chance to
ride their Jeep on the bus to the remnants of forests where
they once spent their living lives.

A list of items needed for this ceremony:

yarrow

breath

skin

a sense of unwavering

cedar

a river rock

a mountain rock

a pair of lucky dice (connected to the others at home
gleaming on the windowsill)

a pause

something found that sparks a keen eye

innate reverence

water

Tina would list fire but it's best to leave some things
at home. In this day and age, with so much of the world
burning, it's better to be so careful with fire. Smoke calls

attention to itself and Tina intends to keep this work quiet. Let it be the work underneath the other work that attends carefully to fear, so it licks intently but does not rupture the borders of elation.

~

Vienna's wet spell before Eloise came back wasn't the longest, but it was the darkest. Dry spells and wet spells, her sisters got to calling them. And Vienna took up that talk too. Tina and Mary-Anne would make food for Vienna's kids when the wet fear would be too much to move through, take them for nights when the dry fear would start talking and she'd be spinning at the mouth all the time, every bad thought that came to her, hurting her kids with her own hurt, weaving them into the bad parts of her story where they didn't belong.

Mama had the stroke and was in hospital and Mary-Anne's pills were not enough to deal with the worry of mama and the wildness of Vienna, who drank herself to oblivion trying to take away the fear pain. Mary-Anne was there but she was having trouble getting out of bed in the morning, and Vince was doing most of the minding. She'd sit by mama's side for hours, unmoving, sunk into the replay of her thought mind, working out the stories for how life would go on for each of them without her, were Mary-Anne just to slip away.

Mary-Anne was thinking about dying and mulling over Vienna and the repulsiveness of elderberry wine, which she learned intimately after she and Vince made a carboy of it, but didn't quite have enough elderberries so mixed in some raspberries from the freezer frozen the year before. The stuff was so sickly sweet it gave Mary-Anne a hangover before she even got halfway through a glass. It was so thick she had to cut it with soda water. Vince tried to convince her age might mellow it out. It didn't, but they drank all twenty-three litres of it anyway. Her sisters helped her through at least fifteen litres of the stuff before she finally decided for good she wouldn't drink with them anymore. Lord knows she could have easily pawned the whole lot off on any one of them, well, maybe not Vienna at the time, because after the first fifteen litres and the night she punched Mary-Anne in the face before disappearing for a week, Vienna declared she was on a dry spell before asking Mary-Anne for forgiveness, holding out her favourite silk scarf with a bit of sage wrapped inside. If it were now, Vienna would have downed as much of it as she could because after mama's stroke she had given in again to the lonely sad bits of the dry that got her into the kind of thinking she always thought she could drink herself out of.

The kind of dry fear that made Vienna feel like she was days into a desert without water, water the only thing driving her, throat parched to glass shards, mouth like a paste of tacky glue.

So cold in the desert night, her inner fire just a bare ember, spirit body needing spirit fire to ignite, keep herself going through this world. Knowing water alone would just freeze, that's how cold her insides were. Dump a good dose of whisky in the first glass, hot wetness to drown out dry nerves.

Which worked for a while, Vienna thinking she could dance the firewater dance without drowning. And oh, how Vienna could dance! On her ups she was something to behold, sequins and red nails, lips so glossy you could see your reflection in them. Always smoke wisps around her light brown face. Black black hair like a horse's mane galloping in freedom of movement. Dark bars with disco balls reflecting red and blue spotlights. Dream Vienna, so potent in her magic all the men hovered in awe of her, women hurrying to the bathroom mirror to touch up, pale in comparison.

Whisky-smoke smell of Vienna, Ô de Lancôme like a binding spell in the drumbeat darkness.

But firewater's got a demon's sense of humour. She doesn't give her dreams out for free. No way Vienna could keep that kind of dancing up without falling—dry fear drowned out by wet fear no longer ablaze, just burning in the acid pit of her stomach. Hangovers hitting so hard she'd get zombie-like for days, then weeks, sometimes years with short in-between nights holding sway with the magic of firewater, most days just drowned out.

⌒

Tina had been in the midst of crafting outfits for the teeny ghost people based on Dolly Parton's "9 to 5" when mama had the stroke. After the intensity of the first days and weeks were over and life settled back into regular routines, Tina felt a keen anticipation of dread holding her hostage in her body — a hot fear of losing mama while her sisters fell apart. Tina would see herself alone, the whole world burning around her. She could not sit still. The only way to lull herself back to warmth from the fire was by turning her thoughts to the teeny ghost people, who asked nothing from her but fine attention to detail and a knack for pairing surprising patterns. She fell into a particularly cozy fugue while recreating the restraining devices Dabney Coleman wore during his entrapment-in-the-bedroom scenes. She became completely absorbed in crafting Dolly's, Lily's, and Jane's getups during what she referred to as "the Reformation" — a series of character-appropriate empowering feminine office-wear pieces intended to transform a workplace made toxic by patriarchal misogyny into a vibrant space of innovative productivity through policies designed around respectful agency and caring collaboration.

Making these outfits in miniature helped keep her mind off things. Made her feel like she could change things. The teeny ghost people got so into it Tina started to realize she had some power over them. Although ineffectual in helping her mother and sisters inhabit the world without the fear pain always gnawing them to ugliness, Tina thought maybe she could work through the teeny ghost people to make things better somehow. She started thinking of Eloise while she sewed. She talked about needing her, about how if she came back, things might get better, wishing only she had some way to find her. She knew the ghost people were listening. She was coming at it sideways. Pretending she wasn't asking, being really passive about it so the teeny ghost people would think it was their idea to bring her back.

When Eloise came back mama was starting to talk again, though the right half of her mouth was unmovable, slurring her speech to near incomprehension. Valerie had not yet regained her vision and the girls were made to understand that she would need permanent care, that she would no longer be able to hold together the threads of their patchwork lives.

Vienna disappeared for two weeks after she visited mama in the hospital with enough drink in her already that the nurses made her leave. She was ready to start a fight on her way out, but when Tina walked in with Vienna's oldest daughter and the girl looked at her mother with so much sadness ringed at the edges with shame to see Vienna fucking things up again, the fight went out of her. Vienna resigned herself to her worthlessness and headed out the door.

She got herself to Vancouver somehow, ending up in hospital with alcohol poisoning and held in detox for three weeks afterward. Because mama was still unstable, no one went to see Vienna this time. There was no one to call her "baby girl" and tell her they were there for her. When Vienna called to tell Mary-Anne where she was and ask about her kids, Mary-Anne let her know she'd had enough.

"Hey Mary, it's me."

"So you're alive then."

"I'm at Vancouver General, in detox."

"Mmm."

"How's mama?"

"What difference does it make to you, Vee? Sober enough for five minutes to feel guilty about being a shitty mom and even shittier daughter?"

"Fuck off, Mary, I don't need your judgement. I just want to know how mama is, and where my girls are staying?"

Mary-Anne wanted Vienna to hurt as much as she was hurting. She hung up the phone without answering. Fuck her, she thought. Let her feel the full weight of her suffering for once.

Vienna tried Tina, but Tina didn't answer.

"Tee, it's Vee, I'm in Vancouver — at the, hospital? I don't have my phone, but can you call the hospital, um, Vancouver General? I want to know how mama is?"

After a long pause, Vienna whispered, "I'm sorry, Tee. Tell my girls I love them."

Eloise moved in with mama. Three months later, when Vienna got out of rehab, she moved into the house with them, taking up her old room in the basement. She wasn't ready to take on the full duties of life, but wanted to be with her family, do what she could. Do it differently this time; take care to come back with intention so she didn't end up in the same place again. Eloise drove Vienna to her meetings, and stayed with her through those hard nights when the dry fear was burning everything up and all she wanted was to drown it. Meeting after meeting. Witnessing other people's pain, baring her own, in a place where folks were braced to hear it. Each of them walking the uneasy ground of afterwards, hoping to find footing on the path. Each of them hoping this time was afterwards, and not just a pause in between tectonic shifts that would see them drowning again when the next quake hit.

Vienna was trying to believe there was a path that could weave between wet and dry, that she could walk in between extremes and watch the fears rearing at her without falling prey. Something else outside of fear always driving her to dance or seek solace in the demon's dangerous spirit play. Teaching her kids words like "healing," and meaning it by the way she was moving through the uneasiness on all sides. Smell of burning sage and cedar replacing the whisky sweetness. Labrador tea with honey now mingling with the incense of the always burning cigarette smoke to transform the Ô de Lancôme to something earthy, giving Vienna a sense of ground. Somewhere her kids could dig. Somewhere they could tend things without fear of having them uprooted. Temper the extremes of fear—not too wet, not too dry, hey, hey, hey—finding meaning in watching what could grow if you weren't always parched and drowning.

Vienna helped Tina with mama's rehabilitation while working on her own. When Valerie would start to get mean, Vienna would take over, because Vienna understood meanness. Eloise had gotten better at being near their suffering without falling apart, but Valerie's meanness was too much for her to bear. She'd never been able to handle it, feeling like she was nothing if mama didn't approve of her. Which was why Eloise had always been so good, always doing what she thought mama wanted of her, until she followed the wind away, Eloise's one irrefutable act of bravery.

⌒

They are calling me home. They are doing it loudly. I hear them cracking through water. Calling me home again. They want me to go, home. I hear them through the thick scent of water; they feel like fragrant hypocrites, wearing me. I don't want to go home.

—Excerpt from Eloise's journal at that place in the valley where white sand water meets water of aching blue

Eloise left and then came back. She went to the place in the valley where white sand water meets water of aching blue. A place her mother had told her about going when she was a girl. Going there was a marker of cyclical time, a seasonal movement toward the world's expression of itself. There's a lot her sisters don't know about where she went when she was gone. How the place where white sand water meets water of aching blue made a home in her, letting her into a world she felt she had been longing for all her life, a world always wafting at the edges of her senses. A world inside a language that the land had co-created with those who came before, a language that had been taken from them, boxed into knowing now through a language embedded in severance, through which she and her sisters struggled to know themselves. A place where magic approached Eloise, and Eloise learned to approach magic.

There is also a lot Eloise won't tell them. A lot she couldn't tell even if she wanted to, so much of that time being wordless. She hovers between them like a dragonfly, all eyes and iridescence, attending to what they need. They don't really see her. She's an illusion. When they try it's like they can't remember the way she was as a child, even the photographs of her seem like they've been tampered with somehow. As though a spirit got between the backing and the glossiness up front and changed things, though you can't quite tell how with your word mind. You glance and then glance again and there's some play in between but when you look good and hard you think it must have been a trick of light the first time because in the solidity of staring, the photographs seem like the same photographs that have always been there in those old black-paged albums with the wire binding and puffy covers. The little white corners mama glued on to hold them in place. Some of the spots just corners now where photographs have been removed and never put back. Mama's perfect cursive in black ink on strips of cut-out lined paper: *Eloise and Tina at the fair, 1987. Baby Vienna at Jeannie's, 1983. Mary-Anne with her friend Beatrice, dressed for church with neighbours, 1984. Eloise, Mary-Anne, Tina, little Vienna, and papa Santa, Christmas 1989.*

The other girls are those bright childhood versions of themselves, spirits so intact it's like they're leaping from the page at you, reminding you that time doesn't just go one way, but is always doing pirouettes and dashes, lumbering alongside the everyday in other everydays that are living along with you, though you don't always notice they're there. Eloise though, her image is skipping somehow and you have to slow to keep her playing straight, like you're walking with a Discman and you have to smooth your movements out to keep Kate Bush from popping in and out of your soundscape, jarring your affect out of presence with your technology and the breath world.

Water everywhere pressing out of the world. Pressing into it. Forming it with its intentions. Playing with light,

reaped into form by heat/cold. Water so loud it drowns out
everything else, washes the senses clean. Ice, foam, spray,
osmic, fresh, potent. Not sitting inside water. Water so loud
everything else drowns out. Precious whooshing in my ears.
smell world exploding with cold constant pouring. I awaken
into vapour, ice, and flow.
— Excerpt from Eloise's journal at that place in the
valley where white sand water meets water of aching
blue

Eloise had left to follow an overwhelming sense that
was always wafting at her from an unknown she knew
she had to know. It took her a long time to go because of
the loudness of sisters and mother. The scent had always
been there, coming with the wind, leaving her that way
too. She could only follow in wind time and their voices
were so loud she would often forget her intentions. Sisters
and mother talking. Telling Eloise how to be. They were
still loud when she left, but the wind stopped stopping,
constantly berating her with the smell of moving water
verging on ice, wrenching her from the binding spell of
sister sound.

She's partway back now, but her sisters never ask about
why or where because they all resent her for having left in
the first place, for not living life in a way that makes sense
to them. There is too much waking in all of their nights, too
much duty in all of their days. And Eloise seems to always

be dreaming. She gets drawn by smells into other worlds. And while they might catch whiffs and crinkle a nose or crack a satisfied smile, Eloise is completely whisked away. Her sisters think her sweet but daft. They do not understand and are not interested in her floating. Plus they are angry that she left when she wanted to and they cannot leave their thick solid lives beholden to men and children. They resent needing her and not being able to be what she might need, not being able to give it even if they did know.

There is fear amidst the sweet smell of water. Fear amidst the lack of it. Fear of the foulest scents that threaten to annihilate the mind. Eloise has had to learn to float amongst the scent messages without being swept by the wind's whimsies in order to stay in one place. And these are wordless dances. Imageless dances. As Eloise breathes she is always wafting amongst intricate scent worlds that cannot be shared among humans, and she is only just barely able to share in these communications with the subtler creatures who smell in these ways alongside her—more beholden to wind than light. Which is why it is strange that her sisters call her dragonfly, imagining her as a being whose eyes are so intricate they brighten the sky, capable of perceiving wavelengths that human eyes must use gadgets for seeing. That they see her this way reaffirms for her the many ways they do not know her. The many ways they do not try to know her difference, just slotting her otherness within their own family metaphors of who she has always been.

In the night dream waters cracked me cold split gave me
mind sight, taught me a

    raucous secret.

They're always, always calling now, even in my dreams. They
learned how to throw their voices into them, in the waters,

    so strong they overthrow scent.

I see these little beings dancing in my nieces' and nephews'
clothes. They're always spitting mad at me. Teasing me and
telling me I'm selfish for leaving.

They stick little pins into my face that leave red welts in the
morning.

They throw scene after scene at me in which

    my sisters and their children drown or are being pursued
    by terrifying men,

    in which my mother lays dying.

    Monsters with the evilest of intentions go for my sisters, eat
    my mother's spirit. The only thing I can do is try over and over
again to save them.

— Excerpt from Eloise's journal at that place in the
valley where white sand water meets water of aching
blue

Eloise left and then came back again. She went to the place in the valley where white sand water meets water of aching blue. She was not the same as when she left but outwardly was the same enough for her sisters not to question who had come back to them. She was still Eloise, albeit more feral. She was always smelling bits of plants and rocks she carried in her pockets. Took whiffs of her sisters to gauge whatever scene she was walking into. The medicines helped her sniff around her sisters' fears, get behind them to something softer. Rocks in her pockets to ground herself to mineral and lichen scent worlds in which she felt grounded—a protective shroud gifted by the valley where white sand water meets water of aching blue.

Eloise learned in her time in the valley how to smell out other people's fears. Subtleties of scenting manifested in the absence of other humans. Away from the overwhelming scents of her sisters and mother and the oppressive scents that seemed to her to emanate from all humans, pulling her directly into their fear worlds, making her unable to do anything but fear in relation, Eloise was finally able to breathe without being overcome. Eloise absorbed the white sand water's teaching, learned to scent in sync with calm pulse of the valley, embedding its oscillations of being deep into the place in her brain where olfactory stimulation transformed into feeling. She went and the land healed her, teaching her to feel at home in her body, teaching her how to smell through the potency of human fearing, to feel the water of aching blue in relation. Glacial, and ancient and dispassionate. Now instead of closing up into balls of misfiring currents in the logjams of other people's neuroses, Eloise's nerves slipped over, under, through, adept at dispersing to rivulets to later reconvene as river where the ground was safe to flow.

The ghost beings taunted her, bringing her back by breaking into her dreams and disrupting her sensual immersion into the more-than-human world. She resisted them as long as she could. During wakefulness they could not reach her, so she started to parse out sleep, practising embodied awareness beyond the neural pathways worn into her brain through decades of interrelational firing. Becoming who she was in the context of *who she was with* and the moods of those dwelling amidst her. In dispersing herself to scent, she was also rupturing the sense of self she had chanced upon by being born Eloise, the third of four sisters in a family held hostage by circumstance, love, and story. She wanted to learn shape outside the terrible parts of the story, the suffering parts that were always wrenching her insides when she walked into her sisters' worlds and worries. To learn how to bear witness to her mother's bitternesses, anxieties, bodily breakdowns triggered by childhood traumas that were no longer even a threat to her. Traumas that had shaped all of their addictive patterns, made it so Valerie and her girls were always seeking out something to get away from the intense uncertainty and boring repetitiveness of now.

Eloise was pulled back by the magic of the teeny ghost people. If Tina had not brought them between worlds and they had not gotten the idea that bringing Eloise back would soothe Tina's fears, help her focus on diverse and elaborate wardrobes for their cunning activities, Eloise might not have come back at all. She returned because the dreams would not let up and her mother had taught her enough about the dream world that she knew the night-mares would not stop if she did not heed them.

The scent fears trickled in her, wafting between stay-ing and going—when she caught wafts of home, she no longer feared ice breaking against stone and the pulver-ized smell of smashed things, instead there were other subtler scents buried beneath the broken insides of things mixed with smoke and beer and whisky smells that left her throat constricted and raw—smells of roast meats and lemon soap, dill pickles and sugar pie, the sleep smells of Vienna's hair, Tina's teenage baby powder deodorant, and Mary-Anne's library books giving off paper must when she opened them to read stories—emergent scents of moments when they had belonged kindly to one another. Lingering scents of her mother and sisters in an all-encompassing love.

The little water fears had altered the properties of the scent fears, freezing and thawing and vaporizing them enough times that Eloise came back differently, knowing how to smell her way out of the scents that wrecked her so she wasn't always trembling between dialectics of fear.

To have compassion for her sisters' weaknesses. To soothe herself out of her mother's disruptions. To recall water moving between states and flow into safety. She knew in coming back that she could not fix them, knew she had to let go of the hope that there might be a way for her actions to make them better. Instead she practised inhabiting space with them outside the polemics of the stories. To stretch the in-betweens out, to be there with them when they were able, to move away from the meanness when it got too much and be elsewhere with herself to do her healing so that she could lend intention to the children when their mothers were in overwhelm. Being aunty Eloise.

~

Little annihilation fears stun her. The ones in which she falls to nothingness. A writhing thing amidst all the needful enterprises of family. Dullest instrument in the world. A knife which you rub and rub and rub against tomato skin, ending up not with diced morsels but a pulpy skin mess, seeds all over the countertop. Recipe a thing they all spit out, looking at her as though she is a maker of revolting mush rather than healthfully balanced family meals.

Mary-Anne brews her own wine and is married to Vince. She wears whatever is given to her. Not understanding how itchy things cause her to behave in peculiar and unhappy ways, how soft things help her actions be softer. Her sisters have learned subconsciously to pass down garments of silk and alpaca, wash-worn jersey and gentle cashmere. Nevertheless, Mary-Anne continues to wear tweed and Icelandic wool, knitting herself thick toques that irritate her forehead and make her furtive. She walks outside scratching at her skin and thinking of the community beehives, how she would like to knock them down and bust them open with the splitting maul, watching the flurry of this desecration rise up and swarm her to non-existence. She wonders how many stings it would take to stop feeling pain.

Mary-Anne is often fearful; it lends her a quiet anxiousness. Unlike her sisters, she does not understand gradients. Even the dullest fears have a sharpness to them, her mind knowing how to hone them. So there is always an anxiousness to her, anxiousness of fear that might come or might not come, there's just no way of knowing. Fear of what's inside and what might trigger that to being. So that even if she's not fearful, she's anxious that she might be soon. She keeps it in her body, debilitating her to angles. She makes other people nervous with her jagged movements. The pain you can always see in her, pinching up her voice. The older she's gotten, the greater the jaggedness. She would forcefully replace everything she has ever seen with knives. She sees sharpness in everything, decorates her house with daggers. Vince wears a lot of thick moosehide garments so that he is not always getting cut up by the sharpness she hides in all the corners of the house.

Her children have grown thick skins and gift soft scarves to soothe her. She is so careful with them, but fears are the untoward gifts of mothers. We mask them with the most remarkable of braveries but the sharp little fears poke through, forever allowing our children to glimpse our secret brokenness. The children don't know that before them, these were not Mary-Anne's fears but their grandmother's. Fears Mary-Anne thought she had outgunned with learning.

It began when she was pregnant with her eldest. These little dreams of dying. She began to think of all the small ways that she might be killed or maimed or broken, leaving her baby alone in the world. In the first few months of infancy, the fears abated. Drowned out by coagulating hormones of love. Long enough after that her sisters were no longer on the lookout for postpartum. Long enough after that she thought it was craziness creeping in. She dreamed they were coming for her and that no one was there to help. *They* were always changing. Sometimes it was even the loveliest of creatures. Tiny squirrels eating nuts and berries who would all of a sudden turn mean. Munching the skin off her face to chew into balls they would stuff in their cheeks and stash in the crooks of dry trees. Her blood-ripped skin drying to hard pellets to dig up in the din of winter. Sometimes unearthed by hungry bears and tasted as pops of iron amidst otherwise planty things. Old ladies with grey hair wearing wool blanket wraps, mashing her with crooked canes carved into the shapes of the animal spirits that were meant to protect her. Voracious men who wrecked her body and left her naked to die. The kind of boys you saw on television who were always portrayed as "good kids" with self-assured smiles and heavy tote bags of privilege that made them think it was okay to take whatever they wanted. Her children would be there all along the edges of the violence, and the only thing she could do to help them was draw the violence toward herself. Make herself the only possible target so that her babies would be left unharmed. As fearful as anything in her sacrifice that they might still be wrecked after she had been irreparably damaged, that her only power would prove to be the most clichéd kind of impuissance.

She did everything to mask these profound weaknesses of motherhood. Mary-Anne, who had been the self-assured sister. Mary-Anne, who had written books about geographies of violence and dispossession, cited throughout with the big names of theorists who knew her work and testified to its poignancy. Mary-Anne, who had a seventh *dan* black belt in tae kwon do, and could, if she needed to, break violence with violence.

Part 2: *The Teeny Ghost People and the Mother*

Before she made clothes for us we were always so cold. It was hard to enjoy ourselves and we were often cranky.

We played mean tricks on the children, like putting toys in front of them when they were running so that they would fall and skin their knees, crying and reaching for their mothers. And their mothers would have to stop what they were doing and comfort them, never getting done the things they needed to get done because of the children's needs. We did whatever we could to make the children fight because their anger warmed us a little. We liked to hide things like keys and corkscrews, and leave the chicken coop door open at night so the fox could get in and feed. A lot of time we took no interest in what people were doing, but every once in a while when the coldness wasn't getting to us as much, we would do something helpful—like ride a blue jay to the window to lift Tina's spirits, or leave out shiny river rocks for the children to find and delight in. Sometimes we asked eagles to shed a feather for Vienna to find, lending her a little bit of power.

It was a trick we were playing on Tina that we didn't think would work the way it did. She was feeling sad about the children's things. Nostalgic about their infancy and the clothes she had loved them in disappearing from her everyday existence to make memories for other mothers, or becoming trash to toss in the landfill if they were too worn to pass on. She was feeling morose and quirky while she went through the children's drawers and made piles of discards, and keeps, and pass-ons. When she went to the bathroom a few of us started messing with the piles, pulling at the holes in things to make the garments tear into pieces that we used as cloaks. The kids had been in bed for a few hours. It was getting near Tina's own bedtime. She had had a few drinks by then, but not too many, so she was feeling rough and playful. We weren't very good yet at understanding how to make the clothes move, but she noticed us doing it—not in the sense that she saw us, but more in the sense that it sparked something in her. She was in a state to see beyond the frustrating mess— her piles askew and things torn up that weren't there the last time she looked. Normally, Tina would have flipped to blame, pinning the frustration on her husband or one of the kids, muttering a bit under her breath at the thanklessness of curating a family's things. But this time it gave her an idea. She took up some pieces and went to her sewing kit. She poured another glass of wine and cut some pieces up into crude dress-like things, then hand-stitched three of them into tunics. She got out her beads and beaded a little flower into each one. The beads made us feel trippy. After Tina had gone to bed we fought all night over who would wear them, and by dawn had come to a sharing agreement, taking turns playing at being pretty.

The one I got to put on was made from giraffe pyjamas that had blueberry stains on them where Tina had beaded in a forget-me-not. When I put it on I felt warm for the first time in forever. Not just the sparks of heat I'd get once in a while from the children's quick madness, but a warmth that seemed to come from the inside, like I had an inside that filled out into something and this something animated the dress in a strange and beautiful way that was almost living. I felt the babies' peaceful sleeps seeping out of the dress into an emergent me. A me that before then hadn't had a sense of self, at least not for a real long time. Tina got up before everyone that morning, and she saw us in the blue light dazzled by this newness of form, moving about on the children's play table in the little dresses. She stood on the stairs and watched without us noticing she was there at first. We had always been around doing things, but until we put on Tina's dresses, no one had ever caught us doing those things. The dresses happened to be just the right size. They happened to have shiny beaded flowers embroidered in them. That was the way the magic worked. A little bit of chance, a little bit of inspiration, a little bit of desire and artistry and the liminality of perception sparked by morning's blue light.

⁓

Valerie does not appreciate the way her daughters are with their children. Except Eloise, who doesn't have any. She would have made a terrible mother. The others aren't that good at it either. They're always trying too hard, Valerie thinks. No wonder they are flying off the deep end half the time. It had been simpler when she was a young mother.

Harder too, in different ways. But simpler. You weren't expected to always be tapped in to every surfacing emotion in your children, to be there to help them feel better every second of every day. They had to learn to deal with things on their own, or help each other out. That's what her girls had done. What would these kids become with all the attention lavished on them? Where did this strange idea come from that you should be friends with your children?

Valerie doesn't want her girls knowing everything about her. She has her private life that is none of their business. Her own sufferings that she has learned how to live with, how to get by in the world despite what was done to her. But they are always asking questions about how she is feeling and who she is seeing and how she is spending her time, and things she could do to deal with her backaches or cough, if she mentions them. They are sure she is lonely and feel guilty about living their own lives and leaving her alone to live hers. Tina always wants to take her shopping to try out old-lady dresses that she doesn't want to wear. It embarrasses her to go into the dressing room and have to come out to show Tina while the saleswomen look on and offer opinions she isn't interested in hearing. Or worse, when Tina goes into the dressing room with her so she can help with zippers and she's yelling at her kids through the door to keep nearby and not jangle the hangers on the racks while making comments about Valerie's "nice waistline" and "still shapely legs."

There had been a few years after Vienna's father died and the girls all left home that had been difficult. She had thought they would have called and written more. Especially Eloise. Eloise was supposed to stay with her. She had said she would. And she was unmarried and childless so she didn't have any real reason not to be with her mother. But Valerie knew that women were supposed to do things on their own now. It wasn't savoury to be with your mother all the time. There were all those books about self-discovery she saw on the shelves at the bookstore. She had tried reading through one about grief and healing after Yan died. She felt like the words were written for other people, not her. Like she would have been putting on airs to start thinking about herself with words like "actualization." She had looked it up and still didn't understand what it meant. She was already real enough, what did she need to go making herself realer for? And to be honest she hadn't grieved him long anyway. It was more that she didn't know what to do with herself after he was gone. In some ways she felt relieved, though she never would have said it, that she didn't have to worry about doing things for him anymore, or about all the things he did that infuriated her. She didn't have to put up with his messes and man smells, things she'd long ago stopped finding charming. The first thing she had done after the funeral was to gather up all his socks and burn them in the oil drum out back. She had put tobacco on the fire too — it wasn't an act of vengeance.

She had wanted to gather up all the pieces he was always leaving scattered around the house, to send them off to the spirit world with hot grace. The kind of grace he never had a chance for while he was living.

Valerie wasn't sure why it was so hard for women these days, but she saw it wasn't only her daughters. The women on TV were doing it too. The TV moms in her sitcoms and tele-dramas. Life was very complicated for them with their full-time jobs and sophisticated fashions, their state-of-the-art homes and fancy dinner parties. The sex they were having with their husbands and lovers, all while driving the kids to soccer practice and fundraising for band trips to London. Imagine that! Sending your kids to blow their trumpets and tenor saxophones on the other side of the ocean! At fourteen! It seemed absurd to Valerie that these were necessary things for mothers and children to do to feel they were living good lives. The TV moms were always going for promotions at work and talking about how to organize their schedules to streamline and maximize work-life balance. They talked about it in tight yoga clothes on their way to the studio with one another while they were texting other people who weren't there about laser hair removal and their children's orthodontist appointments. It made Valerie tired. Still, she watched them doing it because it was a way to spend her time now that she couldn't move around as much, and the storylines were interesting. There weren't any shows about women like her on the TV anyway. And even though the TV women were more put together than her daughters, she felt they helped her understand her daughters better. Her other daughters, not Eloise. She was something different. They gave her ideas for what to say to the girls when they talked about their problems, which seemed different from what her problems had been. Because her girls had been educated in ways she hadn't. Though she knew plenty of things they didn't know. Different and similar too, mother things. She hadn't thought about them as problems, not really. They had just been her lot. The things she had to struggle through. Just like everyone else had their lots, and some folks had it harder than others and you had to be thankful for not having it worse. But her girls, it seemed like they felt the world owed them something. Like if they weren't collecting every minute of their lives on this promise, that they were being cheated somehow.

Had she taught them that? By making life too easy for them? What would it be like for their kids then?

Sometimes her daughters tried to bring up things about their childhoods that they were still blaming her for. But she hadn't done things to them that were done to her. Or let other people do things to them. She had done what she could. She couldn't have done better. So why were they blaming her for their problems? They were ungrateful and still felt they had a right to say how she should live her life. Coming up with ideas for where to put her and how she should spend her time. Like this was what daughters should be doing. Eloise never said these things, but maybe she would have too if she had done things the way the other girls had? The way women were supposed to do things now. And now it was worse because there were so many things Valerie couldn't do for herself anymore. She hated to ask, especially to the other girls, but at least to Eloise she didn't feel like she was begging. Because at least Eloise listened to her instead of always getting mad and taking things personally like the other girls. She didn't always do what Valerie said, but at least she listened.

Now Valerie was glad Eloise didn't have kids and a husband to distract her, but for some years, Valerie couldn't see her as anything but sad. She had even encouraged Eloise to find a husband, and worried about her that she hadn't and didn't seem like she would. She understood now that had been a mistake. Eloise wasn't cut out for it. And Valerie saw the other girls needed Eloise to be the way she was to keep them together now that Valerie couldn't do it anymore. She didn't have the energy for it, for keeping it all straight in her mind. All the checking in and figuring out of different versions of the story getting told by each of the girls. Not so bad right now because Vienna wasn't drinking, but you could never be sure how long that would last and it would be back to the angry phone calls with different pieces of information about how Vienna was mad at Mary-Anne for taking her kids and yelling at Tina on the phone and Tina was calling Valerie to see if she knew where Vienna was because no one had heard from her in two days.

Valerie didn't even have a cell phone or the internet then so she would probably be the last one to know when Vienna showed up again, unless she came over and slept in her old room, which she did sometimes when she was trying to sober up. Or having to call Mary-Anne to see if she had the kids or if Tina did those years Eloise was away and Vienna would be there in the morning with a black eye and smelling of whisky and that perfume she always wore. Not sure if Mary-Anne was in one of her depressions or not and whether Tina would be there to help out or if she was over her head and Valerie would be left with all the grandkids and later the girls would get mad at her for not feeding them the things they did and letting them watch too much TV.

And then the husbands. Tina's husband, Cam, so upright and sure of himself it was like ice coming off him whenever he was nearby. Always telling Valerie how she should fix things up around the house, or suggesting she get a cleaner in the once or twice a year he came over — though he did appreciate her cooking, ate like Tina wasn't feeding him at home, the only time he melted a little was when he had warm meat or sugary treats softening on his tongue. Vince was okay. Quiet mostly, he did what he could to help Mary-Anne, but he had his own issues and would just walk away when it got too much sometimes, the way men did. He always came back, but it meant Valerie had to be there for the grandkids, even when she didn't want to. She knew if she wasn't what would happen. She knew social services would step in if she didn't. Every once in a while the social workers showed up to ask questions, different ones every time, most didn't last long in the community. She always acted like a happy grandma then: "Room for everyone," she'd say. No, she didn't know where Vienna was, but Vienna had asked her to take the kids for a while, she'd tell them, even though Vienna would be sleeping it off downstairs.

But Vienna had been sober for almost a year this time. She was doing things differently. No men around. "No more men," she said. After they chased the last husband off. She had also said "Third time's a charm," but it hadn't been. Far from it. Far from a charm, that one. What had his name been? Chris? No, Krist! For Christ's sake! Krist! Vienna was always correcting her. "With a *t*, Mom!" At least she hadn't had any kids by that one.

~

The teeny ghost people brought Eloise back when her family needed her. Sometimes, if we're lucky, aunties come back after they go away for a while. If they've gone away for their own reasons and haven't been dragged away by addiction or violence. If they've gone to a place in the mountains where the water is at its loudest and the teeny ghost people figure out how to use vapour and clouds and dreams to get to them and call them back. It's a lot harder to come back if your mind and body are caught up in other ghosts. Hungry ghosts that don't stop gnawing. The teeny ghost people don't have the kind of power in this story to break that kind of spell, even though we wish they did. It was not the ghost people that brought Vienna back and helped her stay sober. They don't have that kind of magic and they don't have the power to bring aunties back from the dead, except in ghost form—but the ghost forms of aunties are not straightforward or easy to understand, and luckily this time things don't go that way, so we don't have to figure out how to understand ghost aunties for this story.

Who knows why the ghost people do what they do. Who knows if it's out of kindness or if Tina made a deal with them. Like, maybe Tina told them that if they didn't bring Eloise back she'd take all their clothes and burn them. Or would stop making outfits that allowed them to fill into themselves and enact the kind of dramas they were really getting into with their wardrobes and the characters emerging through them. The kind of dramas they never imagined when they were all muddled in their ghostliness and just able to play tricks or fizzle in and out of presence.

Tina was able to intimate a favour because the garments gave the teeny ghost people materiality and it made them feel good. Their desires got a bit pointed. They had other desires too, but for this story it's only the ones related to the garments and the sisters that are important for us to know. Plus, ghostly desires are tricky to spell out in words. They're rackety and spooky, like shivers up spines and hairs on necks. Subtle cringes through subtle nerve fibres. Wind-licked embodiments of mostly untenable otherworlds. Sister desires are clearer. Sisters want all their sisters nearby. They want their sisters to be happy, but not too happy, so their sisters' lives do not seem so much better in comparison to their own. Sisters want their sisters to help them out when they need to be helped, and for their sisters to laugh a lot alongside them and not hurt too much. Sisters want their sisters to be the aunties the kids need, and to fill out their parts of the stories.

~

We wanted more clothes and got Tina to make them. She got all up in art feelings by doing it. It got so that she would walk around looking at textures and patterns and thinking about us and how we'd feel if she made us garments embroidered with lichens and beads made out of hollowed-out bits of cedar painted with the changeability of clouds. She felt rebellious somehow, cutting up her daughter's favourite dresses and using them to make things for us. At first the girl was upset about it, but she liked the getups Tina made for us and got into it eventually. Tina would let her pick out ensembles and although she was not allowed to touch the ones she made for us, she'd make similar ones for her to play with, with her dolls and stuffies. Tina even showed her how to make stitches so that the girl could make her own. The girl was never as happy with the crude dresses she made as the intricate ones Tina made, and even though she whined and complained about hers not being good enough, Tina encouraged her to keep trying, talking to her about patience and learning while demonstrating her craft. The girl liked the praise her mom gave her for trying and noticing the way things might fit together, so she kept at it. We tried a few times to animate the girl's designs, but it just didn't work with what she put together the way it worked with what Tina created.

We're not sure what will happen when Tina isn't able to make clothes for us anymore. Either we'll wear what she's made for us until it disintegrates back to earth and we frazzle back into immaterial ghostliness, or we'll enact preservation policies that are intended to keep the pieces safe from the degrading qualities of time. Worn only for ceremonial purposes—ceremonies designed in relation to the pieces, imbued with symbolic motifs that get transfigured through generations as Tina's original intentions become transformed through our own interpretations. Centuries after the cultural signifiers that lent Tina's creations spark have fallen away, we'll work with our own remembered stories and contemporary familial contexts to enliven our garbs.

Or maybe the girl will get the magic somehow. Through some apprenticeship and learned mastery. Maybe there needs to be mastery and kinship ties for the magic to come through? Maybe it's an ancestral magic that was waiting for Tina to happen upon it, skilled enough in her craft to intuit her way into it. Maybe that's why we keep hanging around all the time in all our trickery and hopefulness. Because we belong to them and they belong to us somehow.

Pooka

Pooka lived in a room with carpets of all shapes and sizes woven from different cloths. Pooka picked up carpets wherever he went. Most of the time unwanted carpets were dirty or cut up or had cigarette burns in them or smelled like cat piss, so Pooka had a lot of cruddy carpets alongside the nice carpets he was gifted or able to buy during blowout sales at home furnishing stores, end-of-the-roll off-sales, and Oriental outlets. He mixed them together because Pooka was like that, all mixed up himself. Off-white blend of kinfolk peppered down the line. Indian nearly fractioned out, they told him, because grandmaman Thérèse, already a half-breed, married Renaud Fortier, a Frenchman from the logging camp upriver. Then mama took up with Gunther Poundsly, Pooka's no-good pa, who gave only bruises, crooked teeth, a penchant for sauerkraut, and armfuls of meanness until he left them to go back to the Sault.

Mama said, "Getting lighter with each successive generation of mixing"; said, "Despite blending in, the ghosts of the ancestors are all frayed up inside, calling to our spirits with directions we don't know how to follow, so we get lost along the way."

Frayed up from not knowing how to live between worlds, Pooka knew—from the structural forgettings legislated on mama and grandmaman's lives, and the oceans between here and the places in the world his other people came from. Mama did some big forgetting, she said, when she was twelve years old and the government came to take her out of the bush, place her in a good white home where there wasn't no more booze, just a whole lot of work, a brother who liked to touch her up, and godliness she shed as soon as she skipped out at sixteen. Didn't see grandmaman again until Gunther left and the city streets spat her out, back to the village with her little boy. Not-quite-white Pooka, picked on at powwow for his white-boy face, ticking the Métis box on the census 'cause that was the closest fit. Never mind that saying it out loud made him feel like a sham, bringing up everything he didn't know about who he was supposed to be.

Pooka felt there was no real demarcation between things. He learned from his school books that life was a mash-up of history told like a storybook of happy endings if you were on the right side and unfortunate circumstances that couldn't be reversed now if you weren't.

He knew that the sullied carpets he collected had been woven from pristine cloth, that given time and human use the new carpets would become sullied. For Pooka, the mixed-up rugs felt something like a homeland. A place to collapse time and storylines, create a sanctified present from a mucked-up past.

The rugs were Pooka's only furnishings. Layered and layered on each other to make a bed or a rise on which to set a coffee mug. Sometimes Pooka got creative and sculpted them into intricate replicas of couches he sat on at other people's houses.

Once, during a particularly bleak winter, he sculpted an entire IKEA bedroom suite. The lampshade was a bit tricky, and although he was usually loath to do so, for this particular project he got hold of a pair of scissors. He cut up one of the already-torn carpets so that the lampshade would fit right and not light on fire from pieces of fabric touching the bulb. He looked up videos of how to wire a lamp on YouTube and scavenged wiring from a lamp of cousin Vicky's. It made Pooka feel modern to have a lamp in his home, to live in an IKEA bedroom suite like all the women he met who worked at smart retail stores, the only ones other than cousin Vicky who would talk to him.

Pooka spent a lot of time in smart retail stores pretending to shop for things. Mostly he was getting ideas for how to sculpt his carpets, or noticing display carpets showing wear that might come on sale sometime soon because no one would want to pay full price for them. Pooka knew how to talk carpet; he could always haggle the saleswomen down. With salesmen he didn't even bother, feeling most of the time like they weren't worth the trouble of talking rug with. They wanted to seal the deal, not send the carpet to a good home. Or so Pooka thought.

Pooka was thrilled when his room of sculpted carpets was featured on a website. One of those sites where people who spend a lot of time on computers go to compare their own lives to those of other people they have never met who live in places like New York or San Francisco. Meaningful places with panache that people might imagine themselves in. Online mock-ups for how to navigate the world of things and properly curate a life. His "eclectic suite," however, was quickly taken down because of the spiteful put-downs posted by viewers who were used to staged, minimalistic homes. Homes that displayed their inhabitants' sophistication, cookie-cutter individuality, and eye for tasteful decor. Homes that had class.

This place looks like a thrift store stocked by a blind four-year-old, wrote Micah4u. *Is this a joke?* posted dEsignBaby. *This is the most tasteless jumble of trash I've ever seen in my life*, was Grendel Piker's response.

Pooka was crushed. This was during his 1960s *Star Trek* phase, when he'd actually gone so far as to spray-paint some of his carpets silver and black to look like the captain's chair.

His photographer friend Peanut, who had taken the artful photos of Pooka's rug replica of the uss *Enterprise* (ncc-1701), felt awful about the ordeal.

Pooka pretended not to care about what online design critics thought of the place he called home. He reckoned they couldn't see beyond the obvious, viewing things only in terms of outlines and not in terms of spirit. He saw that theirs was a gated community of taste, that they used aesthetic condemnation to keep the riff-raff out. Nonetheless, Pooka dismantled the carpet rendition of Captain Kirk's bridge.

Until then Pooka's fanciful successes in carpet sculpture had helped to keep his mind off mama's latest disappearance, let him keep pretending she was just drifting, that like every other time she had drifted before, she would find her way home. But time stretched on and mama did not resurface. With nothing to distract him, Pooka knew this time that mama was lost, the way tante Bernadette was lost, and Tina from high school, and Liz from the village upriver. No follow-up down at the station, no mention on the evening news or photos along the roadside. One more woman washed out of a world scripted to efface her, not even a ripple in the surface of the fabricated story in which all people belong.

Pooka's online ridicule was one more disappointment in a life he could only see through his sorrows. Alone on the outskirts of his humanity, not belonging became too much for Pooka. He ceased pretending to be Mr. Spock, wearing pointy ears and trying all sorts of foreign foods he found around town to test the Vulcan's taste buds. He couldn't remember what grandmaman had said about always being at home among his ancestors because he could not speak their tongues and had no sense of the inspirited landscapes they'd inhabited. He could not hear them because they were far gone to him, people in history books wearing clothing crafted from animal skins, weaving baskets and boxes from plants. Pioneers with fringe jackets and musket rifles, bottom-of-the-barrel Englishmen sailing in the bowels of dank ships, German peasants tilling up whatever land they could find, uprooting hundred-year-old trees with bare hands.

Pooka's sneakers were made in China by labourers he'd never know, his skin clothed in factory cotton travelled all around the globe, while he'd barely been a hundred klicks from the one-room box he called home. Unlike grandmaman, Pooka couldn't hear the ancestors when he walked through the furniture district downtown built atop the old fish camps. But sometimes Pooka imagined that the carpets gave voice to them, that the foreign-made rugs hoarded up in showrooms scattered all over the city might be a medium through which the relations could speak. The IKEA suite and the bridge of the *Enterprise* were Pooka's attempts at coaxing them out.

After Pooka's online ventures in "carpArtry" were quashed, and with mama gone for good this time, he became unable to feel at home among his carpets. For five years Pooka kept things flat. He didn't shop around or notice shifting trends in rug manufacturing. He lost track of developments in loom engineering and stopped haggling for deals altogether. Pooka was down-and-out. During these years Pooka worked on and off as a casual labourer for various construction projects. He experimented with crystal meth and got addicted to it, the way people do. He made other meth friends who were down-and-out like him. A lot of scattered spirits stimulated only by the hit, every other aspect of life losing texture, ceasing to impart meaning.

His den became littered with drug paraphernalia, unwashed dishes, and dirty laundry he couldn't bother to clean. Pooka lost sense of himself. He couldn't find space in his heart for the things that had once fed him, even though he finally had a girlfriend who cooked for him: bowls of pasta with sauce from a jar and broken light bulbs of crystal. Poor little messed-up Mel, who burst into fits of rage when his attention went elsewhere.

When he wasn't high, and often when he was, Pooka laboured on the infrastructure for modern condos downtown, making sure to always leave jobs before getting to the interiors. Pooka didn't want anything to do with the insides people would inhabit. He always took special care not to go into the show suites because of the shame they brought up in him about his loss of inspiration. Because they highlighted how clean people would live, people who weren't like him and couldn't understand the depths of his degradation, his loneliness, and all the ways he'd been hard done by in this world. Never-loved-properly Pooka crouching inside the cupboards, papa smashing pots overhead in the sink, muttering about his uselessness.

Things would have gone on like this if it weren't for the special set of circumstances that sheared the fuzz from Pooka's synapses. They would have gone on like this until desperation led to violence, incarceration, bodily breakdown, or just plain giving up. Pooka was often up in the ironworks; it would not have been difficult to fall. Only the thought of his carpets kept him from inching off the edge, the thought of the voices trapped up in them that might be lost forever if he didn't arrange them into perceivable forms. Pooka knew for certain they'd be thrown into a trash bin by his landlord, who would find them filthy, even cringe at the thought of them, when he'd recount the story of having to haul out Pooka's decrepit stacks.

It was a deconstruction project in the warehouse district on the industrial fringes of the city that finally bridged Pooka's mind and heart. A complex of concrete blocks that had been abandoned and boarded up since before Pooka had moved to the city. The faded lettering on the awning illegible in the grimy expanse of a neighbourhood you only went to if you had something specific to get at one of the duct ventilation or fire safety supply stores.

Pooka walked into what was once Desislava's Authentic Eastern Imports gritty and wanting, his heart like the sandpaper tongue of a mother cow licking flies off her just-weaned calf across the wire, risking the electric shock to get some closeness. Frazzled, murky Pooka, just this side of the meth binge that had started as a helluva time but finally broke him and Mel, leaving him friendless on the other side.

Pooka didn't notice what was all around him in the dim light until he felt a full-bodied cushioning rise up through the soles of his steel-toed boots. He started, recognizing the somatic resonance of a nineteenth-century Chiprovtsi kilim. He dropped to his knees to examine the fibres, running his labour-roughened hands along the weft of the red and black threads. Pooka knew this was authentic Bulgarian, could sense in the filaments an outpouring of nationalistic sentiment from just after the Crimean War. He looked up and saw an entire storeroom of rolled and stacked rugs, dotted here and there with statuettes, vases, and urns, coated with rubble from the collapsing roof and dank from water damage at the southeast end. Pooka woke up, snapped into consciousness as if charged by an electric current running through an otherwise inert substance.

He returned to his being amidst Desislava's abandoned relics, receptors in his brain sensing joy from something other than methamphetamine for the first time in years.

"The whole lot of it's for the dump," said Boss Slims, who'd hired him to do the job.

There on the kilim, Pooka sensed he'd been called upon to salvage what he could of the ruins of Desislava's treasures, precious emblems of foreign cultures cast upon his shores. He asked Slims if he could take some of the wreckage home instead of tossing it out.

"So long as you ain't turning a profit I don't see no issue with it," said Slims. "I got the call from city hall to haul it to the trash yard before they tear it down. Don't see as anyone would mind you sifting through, so long as there ain't anything shady you intend to do with it."

He paused and Pooka twitched, both from anxiety— that he might have to resort to criminal pillage to take the kilims home if Slims didn't agree to it—and the neurotoxic effects of meth withdrawal.

"There was some kind of scandal that ended this place up in the courts some while back, so it might be someone's keeping an eye out," Boss Slims recalled.

"It was in the papers but I can't recollect the details, maybe deportation or tax fraud. No one could liquidate 'til they cleared up the ownership. In '97 or '98 we got that real bad winter with the ice storms and frost heaves, come spring there was a crack clear through the back wall.

Water's been seeping for years, no one allowed in to do anything about it. All this junk left to rot. Mould and rat shit all over the place. Can't see there's anything worth anything left, but you might find something worth keeping. Must've been a fortune here at some point."

Pooka told Boss Slims it was for an art project. Slims looked at him cockeyed, unsure about the kind of art Pooka'd make out of this mess. He told him to be discreet, not to go showing things off or anything, seeing as someone might recognize the material if they were looking for it. Pooka said he'd be selective, dump most of what was there like he was supposed to, and transform what he took beyond recognition so no one could trace things back.

___

Pooka lives in a room lined with carpets of all shapes and sizes and colours woven into different forms. Six years Pooka's had with the detritus of Desislava's big dreams. Six years keeping himself clean by tending to the discards of someone else's life and in so doing reimagining his own. Pooka has moved beyond stacking now, daring to dream beyond the confines of an inherited reality. Pooka unravels threads and weaves new images, reinterpreting the past. In the new tapestries, Pooka's mama lives in a nest edged by curlicues and red-leafed maples. She comes and goes as she pleases and no harm can reach her. He weaves her as a hawk, like in the stories she used to tell him. Pooka remembers that mama loved him once, before a bad life got hold of her spirit, broke her wings, and boxed her into a story she could not live out.

Pooka is joyful for mama, joyful to tell her story the way she wanted it told. He drapes her on his back and carries her to the shore to watch the waves come in, to be held in by her ancient warmth.

The act of unravelling releases the knots that ruptured the ancestors' storylines, fraying them up so that Pooka could not hear them, could feel only the schism of loss. Pooka's whole being is immersed in the work of untangling, and even though he doesn't always know what the voices of the ancestors are saying as he takes apart and remakes, he hears their joy and is able to feel hope. They come to him as if in dreams, ancestors who feel the wind in their hair, haul fish up from the river, same river out the window, same water that wetted the ancestors' tongues, upon which they travelled. Pooka envisions the wind, allowing it to tickle the water; frissons of blue, green, and white dotted here and there with the bright silver flashes of fish coming home, souls waiting to be reborn. Streaks of grey and brown amid the red and yellow flush of autumn, faces open to the wind as they transition between this life and the next, passing through death along the way.

This form, this life, the structure of reality that smashed him up on the inside, made his mother-folk fade in and out. Made the world a mismatch of other people's stories he could not claim as his own, his father-folk a frenetic aching coursing through his fingers. Pooka sees the holes and loops and presses love into them, easing the passage to rooms where people talk and their voices are the clacking sounds of branches and migratory birds, kinships of forest, field, fowl, fingers tapping out a tune.

Pooka builds bridges between heartbreak and happiness. Bridges to cross over his fear. Safe passage for a cluttered soul hiding out to escape the bang-up job papa did on his life, the system always pressing in to keep him down. He guts the gutters where he's lived so long among the effluents of a world that doesn't want him. He finds brethren there and gives them new forms. As he re-stories rugs, Pooka becomes a maker of worlds instead of a castoff living within the confines of his shame. Reworking threads reroutes his neural pathways. Bit by bit new patterns emerge, healing wounds rather than wearing them raw over and over and over again.

Pooka gathers plants in city parks, along sidewalks, and in the forest edging the ends of bus lines. He lends colours to bleached-out strands: alder bark and wild carrot root for orange, blackberries for purple, lichens for red and yellow, birchbark for brown. He uproots beets from the community gardens to coax a deep red, fixing the dye with vinegar from packets picked up at A&W. Blacks he gets from walnut hulls, staining his hands at the same time, and greens from nettles and peppermint that he also brews into tea. Plants, creatures, and new geographies of colour teach him to sing the songs of the city as his ancestors learned to sing the songs of the land.

Still, this is not a success story to print in magazines read by all the women who work at smart retail stores. Pooka has not remade his identity and turned his life around to become a better version of himself. He has not stepped out of destitution into a life of blissful hope. Despite his efforts, Pooka's threads sometimes lead to despair. His ancestors' sufferings and cruelties, mama's missing face smiling at him from tattered photographs, tante Bernadette, Tina, papa's big fists, and all the traumas of life are there in the mouldy patches of Desislava's rugs. Are there in the morning when he wakes up and everything he loves has been distorted into ugliness or taken from him, hindering his heart. Pooka is often unable to build the bridges needed to traverse his emptiness. Sometimes the way out is not clear. The old ruts in his mind are mighty worn and he longs for a simple wormhole of dopamine to flood him into peace. Even though time after time these quick clicks to happiness have only led to the same sad place.

Pooka tricks himself into presence by delving into the enlivened materiality of the kilims. String by string he weaves himself into place, his fingers unravelling the fabrics of other official histories. He finds hope there for other ways of telling. He'll tie one knot, make a loop, cut here, and the fray of the thread will suggest another pattern. This is no ideal world, fabric constrained by the genesis of its being and former lives, but what is woven can be teased apart. Pooka tampers and tugs at reality, drawing it by hand, creating new pathways through the made-up world.

Author's Note

Memory arises in "Home (in Four Parts)" was inspired by Lee Maracle in *Memory Serves*.

Acknowledgements

Most of these stories were written on Gitxsan Territory, where I am privileged to live and learn. Thank you to all the beings—human and more than human—who bless me with learning as I walk in the world. Thank you to all those who have cared for and continue to care for the land upon which I make home.

I acknowledge my mother, Nicole Lalonde, and my father, Guy Champagne, for creating the first home I knew, and for imbuing that home with love and passion, curiosity and playfulness, and all the other stuff that shaped my earliest knowing. Thank you to my sisters and first playmates in imagination, Belle Aube, Marie-Soleil, Catherine. I am not me without you. And thank you to their children, who made me Matante, which is such an honoured thing to be, Maïa, Solomon, Maisie, Bijou, Venture, Birch, and Yarrow. Thank you to my own children, Philomène and Louvel, and my partner, Lynden—my most poignant teachers in the subtle beauties and complexities of home and love. Thank you to my ancestors and those not yet born. These stories are an alignment of my being toward yours.

So much gratitude to my extraordinary agent Stephanie Sinclair.

Gratitude also to the team at House of Anansi Press for bringing this book to form, especially Michelle MacAleese and Maria Golikova for the deep work with words and process, and Alysia Shewchuk for taking one of my collages and making it speak.

Thank you to Fabienne Calvert Filteau for being such an integral part of this process; your love for my work gives me courage. Thank you also to my dear friends and earliest readers, Sheryda Warrener, Trudi Lynn Smith, Suzanne Ross, Melissa Cowper-Smith, Phillip Maisel, Jessica Ziakin-Cook. Thank you to Andi Schulz and Erley Combs for gardening alongside me and so much more. All of you have shaped me with your creativity and beautiful spirits. Thank you also to Margo Matwychuk, who helped guide the direction of my seeking for many years. And to Laura Eustace and Benjamin Laurie who lent me their quiet home to write uninterrupted for a precious handful of days.

So much heartfelt gratitude to Katherena Vermette for mentorship, support, and encouragement as I learn to bring stories into the world.

Thank you to early readers for encouraging others to read.

Thank you also to the Banff Centre for support to attend the Emerging Writers Intensive in 2019, and to the rad cohort of writers I was so fortunate to be amongst in a time of togetherness before now. I hold that time hearing your stories close in my heart. And thank you especially to Yen Ha for continuing to share words with me.

Thank you to the jurors of the Journey Prize, Carleigh Baker, Catherine Hernandez, and Joshua Whitehead, for seeing something in "Pooka" that was worth noticing. And thank you to the Writers' Trust for financial support to keep writing.

Thank you to *PRISM international* and the wonderful editors there for first publishing my work, and to also to *grain*, *Room*, the *Malahat Review*, *Prairie Fire*, and *Mom Egg Review*, where some of the stories in this book first appeared.

A heartfelt thank-you to Elizabeth Larsen for walking to the river with me and taking photos, and to Kesia Nagata for taking photos of my artwork to translate to digital for the cover. Also a shout-out to @GITX̱SANBUSHGIRL for the earrings peeking out in my author photo.

Thank you to all the writers and seekers whose words have shaped my tellings. There are so many of you, and I feel so much gratitude that my words will also be part of the story.

Lastly, thank you to John Black, Jobe, and Frankie, blessed creatures who shaped the contours of my walking by sensing beyond my knowing and sharing some of that knowing with me as I walked. I miss you.

Photo credit: Elizabeth Larsen

ANGÉLIQUE LALONDE was the recipient of the 2019 Writers' Trust McClelland & Stewart Journey Prize, has been nominated for a National Magazine Award, and was awarded an Emerging Writers Intensive at the Banff Centre for Arts and Creativity. Her work has been published in numerous journals and magazines. Lalonde is the second eldest of four daughters. She dwells on Gitxsan Territory in Northern British Columbia with her partner, two small children, and many nonhuman beings. She holds a Ph.D. in anthropology from the University of Victoria.